Hot Cakes Book Five

Paige Asher likes her men the way she likes her coffee: hot, slightly sweet, and only to-go.

The hot friend-of-a-friend she had a scorching single night with was just about perfect — tall, rugged, with a sexy drawl... and on the road out of town by six a.m. the next morning. Long before her mom could start picking out wedding flowers.

But now she can't stop thinking about the Louisiana boy. His texts make her smile and she suddenly has a craving for gumbo all the time... hot and spicy and far from home.

Mitch Landry had no idea Iowa would be so hospitable to a visitor. He knew the Midwest had a reputation for friendliness but his welcome gift — a sassy, sweet blond who is as no-strings-attached as he is — was a dream come true six months ago.

But why is he still texting her? And why did he jump at the chance to come back to Iowa? And why is he so annoyed by her phobia to commitment this time? And why is he pretty sure leaving Paige this time is going to be one of the hardest things he's ever done?

Damn, is this what falling in love feels like?

Oh, fu... fudge.

The Series

One small Iowa town.
Two rival baking companies.
A three-generation old family feud.
And six guys who are going to be heating up a lot more than the kitchen.

Sugarcoated
Forking Around
Making Whoopie
Semi-Sweet On You
Oh, Fudge
Gimme S'more

Oh, Fudge

NEW YORK TIMES BESTSELLING AUTHOR

ERIN NICHOLAS

One

He had the best hands. Big, hot, slightly callused, causing a delicious drag over her skin. And confident. This guy knew what he was doing when he put his hands on a woman.

His big palm slid up the side of her thigh to her hip, then under the edge of her half sweatshirt onto her bare skin. The hot touch made her suck in a quick breath and then let it out in a soft moan as he ran his hand up and down her ribs.

As his hand was moving, so was his mouth. He dragged his jaw along her neck to her collarbone, the scruff on his face abrading her skin and sending goose bumps dancing joyously down her arms and tightening her nipples.

"Paige."

She loved the way he said her name. Low and needy. The deep voice combined with the slow Louisiana drawl made heat pool in her belly and then slide lower, making her feel achy and tingly. In spite of the fact that she was wearing loose, soft, comfortable yoga clothing—a sports bra, a half sweatshirt that hung off her shoulder and had been washed so many times it felt like cashmere, satiny soft leggings, no panties so as not to pinch or restrict any motions, and nothing on her feet—she was aware of every bit of her clothing rubbing and pressing and she wanted to tear them all off. She *needed* to be naked. She needed to be free to wrap herself around him and feel every inch of him against every inch of her. She wanted his hot skin and his possessive hands and his wet mouth and—

"Paige!"

That wasn't a deep moaning sound. That was a sharp whisper.

Paige's eyes snapped open.

Piper Barry, a friend and one of the women in her afternoon yoga class, was staring at her with wide eyes.

Paige abruptly came back to the moment.

And the yoga class she was teaching. Or that she was *supposed to be* teaching.

Damn. She'd gotten caught up in dirty daydreams about Mitch Landry.

Again.

She never did that. *Never.* Guys were fun, no doubt about it. She loved guys. She loved the things she did with guys—and no, she didn't mean sex. Okay, she didn't *just* mean sex. She did love sex. But she also loved dancing and... okay, she loved men for sex and dancing. Still, that wasn't *just* sex.

But she didn't *daydream* about men when they weren't around.

She cleared her throat and straightened her spine. No more prolonged periods of meditation. She needed to kick this class up a notch. Take her mind off Mitch. And the fact that he was going to be here in two days. After not seeing him for six months. And four days.

She also *never* kept track of how long it had been since she'd seen a guy.

Of course, all the guys she typically saw for sex and dancing she could see any time. For the most part. They didn't live a thousand miles away in another state like Mitch did.

That was probably it. She just wanted what she couldn't have.

The sexy, sweet texts didn't help though. And the fact that the one night they'd had together had been the hottest she'd ever had. And the fact that—

Piper cleared her throat.

Right. Yoga. And the fourteen people facing Paige at that very moment waiting for her next instruction.

"Deep breath in. Feel your ribs rise," she said in her soothing I've-got-your-peace-and-enlightenment-right-here voice. And as if she hadn't been having them sit and quietly center themselves for the past several minutes. And as if her heart wasn't racing and her nerve endings weren't popping and her brain wasn't full of rugged, big-handed, slow-smiling, how-about-you-bend-over-the-end-of-the-bed-so-I-can-hold-on-to-that-sweet-ass-while-I-fuck-you Louisiana-boy thoughts.

Paige shook her head and forced herself to move her class, and *herself*, through the next three poses without any thoughts of how great dirty talk was when done with a soft drawl.

Paige moved them from their beginning sitting pose to their stomachs and then into their first standing pose.

She caught Cam McCaffery eyeing Whitney Lancaster's butt appreciatively.

She could understand how it might be distracting having your girlfriend in yoga class.

If Mitch were here, bending over, or behind her watching *her* bend over... Paige wobbled as her thoughts drifted again, and she pulled in her core and forced her mind onto her practice.

She *loved* yoga. She never had trouble concentrating like this. She looked forward to her practice so she could block out all of the thoughts racing around and the distractions that grappled for a hold on her attention. She was a master at blocking it out. It was why she'd gotten into yoga in the first place.

"Pull your navel toward your spine. Roll your shoulders forward, up, and back. Hug your elbows in, and squeeze your shoulder blades in, together, and down."

Her life in tiny little Appleby probably didn't seem stressful to anyone looking at it from the outside. Appleby was a sweet Midwestern town where everyone looked out for each other. Local businesses were supported. Neighbors brought casseroles over when someone was sick or a family member died. There were town festivals—including the Apple Festival starting tomorrow—and holidays were not just family events but entire community celebrations.

Paige's family had lived in Appleby for generations. Her sister Josie lived in the house that their great-great-grandparents had built when they'd first come to Appleby.

All of that was why Paige did yoga. And collected cats. And drank vodka cranberries.

A lot of cats. And vodka cranberries.

"Now inhale, lift, and lengthen up through your spine," she coached softly and steadily.

Fred, a big, long-haired, orange cat, came strolling past her mat and stopped to have his head scratched. Which she did while still holding her pose, engaging her core, and breathing. The cats were part of the practice, and everyone who came to Cores and Catnip knew they'd be joined by feline classmates.

The cats lounged and watched. Or wound their way between participants, getting petted and cooed over. Sometimes they'd choose a mat and join one class participant for the duration. Sometimes they made their rounds. Sometimes they slept and sometimes they played.

The yoga studio was a cat café and adoption center as well. Actually, Paige's business had *started* as a cat café and adoption center. People could come in, get coffee, smoothies, and healthy treats—oatmeal, multigrain bars, cereal mixes, and low-fat muffins —and work or read with a cat curled up by their feet or in their lap. She ran a used-book swap and offered free Wi-Fi. It had been a great idea. People especially found it interesting since her sister worked at the local bakery, Buttered Up, a business that had been a part of the town for more than fifty years. Buttered Up offered all the typical treats—cupcakes, full-fat muffins, cookies, scones, and pies. Josie was a master baker and decorator. Buttered Up's offerings were absolutely delicious. And a sharp contrast to the food that Paige offered. But she and Josie had fun with it, and recently Josie had started her own side business and now made healthy muffins and bars for Paige as well.

That was just one example of how her family was interwoven into everything Paige did. She loved and hated it.

Her family was here. Everywhere. All of them. All the time. She couldn't run an errand without running into someone she was related to. She couldn't go to the doctor's office without her family knowing—her aunt was the head nurse. She couldn't even dance with a guy without her mother wondering if it was serious and telling her how nice his grandmother/sister/mother/aunt/cousin was. Or how bitchy his grandmother/sister/mother/aunt/cousin was. Sometimes a girl just wanted to *dance* and for it to have nothing to do with his female family members' dispositions.

Actually, a lot of the time a girl just wanted to dance with a guy without involving their families and the fact that his mother once hit her mother in the face with a dodgeball in PE class. On purpose. Or the fact that his aunt was the best Sunday school teacher her sister had ever had.

As if those were reasons for her to get involved, or not get involved, with a guy.

But this was what she lived with. She couldn't have the doctor check her for a rash without her mom and grandmother calling. She couldn't grab a low-fat yogurt without her dad telling her she needed to worry less about her weight and that she should just have a steak or burger once in a while. And since her apartment was upstairs from her yoga studio, heaven forbid someone park their truck along the curb overnight. She'd absolutely have family members asking about who had spent the night and picking up bridal magazines from the bookstore.

This was all absolutely why she did yoga. And collected cats. And drank.

"Keep the bright and energetic lift. Focus on your foundation. Awareness in that front foot," she encouraged, checking on the class. "Hips level. Then lift that back leg slightly."

Why was she thinking of all of this now though? She could always push all of that out of her mind.

But it was like Mitch had wedged open the door she normally shut and locked while she practiced, and that little crack was letting all kinds of thoughts sneak in.

She couldn't wait to see him. She almost wished that he *hadn't* texted to let her know he was going to be in town again. He could have just shown up and surprised her. That probably would have been better.

She wouldn't have spent the last couple of days cleaning her apartment and shopping for food that he could eat while they were holed up together—he did *not* seem like the tofu and edamame type—and juggling her schedule and coming up with lies to tell her mother and various other relatives when they wanted to know why she wouldn't be at the Apple Festival on day three.

She wasn't going to tell them that she intended to spend day three in bed. All day. Naked. Wrapped around a hot Louisiana boy who turned her insides to pudding and made her smile stupidly over his texts as if she were in high school again.

Without warning, she would have just rolled with it the way she usually did when a certain feeling or mood struck her. He could have put up with her dust bunnies and could have gotten food to go from downtown, and she could have just left him in bed to go teach a class or two.

Except leaving him would have been *very* difficult.

"Elongate from the top of your head to your tailbone," she reminded the class. "Then reach."

Bernie, the gray-and-white, short-haired cat, jumped up on the windowsill next to Paige and meowed before yawning widely.

She smiled at him and reached to scratch under his chin. She had to really stretch, pulling in her lower stomach, breathing, and challenging her balance to give him the love but that was one way the cats were such a fun part of the yoga classes. Just having them around also made people smile more, and it was scientifically proven that spending time with animals brought blood pressure and stress levels down.

Paige heard someone clear their throat and with her fingers still grazing Bernie's chin, she glanced toward the door.

Her eyes went round, both arms dropped, and her back leg dropped while her supporting leg gave out. Her brain just stopped keeping her upright. All of her mental energy was immediately focused on the man in the doorway.

She fell to the mat, and the entire room gasped and dropped their poses as well.

Piper was beside her a moment later. "Paige! Oh my God, are you all right?"

Mitch is here! He's here! Early! Already! But he's right over there! Yay! Gimme!

But she simply pushed her hair back and gave Piper a smile. "Yes, of course. Bernie threw me off-balance."

Piper eyed the cat who was still on the windowsill, now licking a paw and looking entirely unconcerned about, well, anything. Typical.

"Did you... hurt yourself?" Piper asked.

"Nope."

The rest of the class was leaning in as if to hear, and Cam and Whitney moved closer.

"I just got a little distracted," Paige said softer. She caught Whitney's eyes, then Piper's, then looked toward the doorway.

Mitch was leaning against the doorjamb. He was wearing faded blue jeans and an olive-green t-shirt that she knew matched his eyes. They wouldn't be able to tell from here but it was exactly the right shade. His hair was a little shorter than the last time she'd seen him, but he still had the short beard and, even more dangerous to her libido, that smirky half smile that said he knew she'd just fallen down because of him.

He wasn't wearing a jacket even though it was January. She assumed he had one. Though it never got all that cold in Louisiana. Not heavy-winter-coat cold anyway. And yes, she'd looked that up. She'd freaking done research about where this guy lived. That was... crazy.

He did, however, have boots on. They weren't exactly winter snow boots. More like scuffed-up work boots. But they'd keep his feet warm while tramping through the six inches of snow that blanketed Appleby currently. One booted ankle was crossed cockily over the other as he leaned against the doorframe watching her unfold herself from her yoga mat.

His arms were also crossed as if he were settled in to watch the rest of the class.

As if their thoughts were connected, his eyes traveled over her as she stretched to her feet again. A flash of heat went through her as he took in what she was wearing.

The same outfit, essentially, that he'd stripped her out of the last time he'd been here.

I love this fucking sweatshirt. The way it hangs off your shoulder, tempting me with these sweet tits right underneath. He'd hooked his finger in the neckline of the sweatshirt and pulled it down underneath her left breast. He'd pulled her bra up and then fastened his dirty-talking, hot mouth right on her nipple.

Now that nipple tingled with the memory and the sight of that mouth just a few feet away.

Piper and Whitney both looked in the direction that Paige was clearly looking.

She grabbed them both, forcing them to look back at *her* before the entire class swung to look at Mitch.

"Don't—"

But it was too late. The other twelve people in the room turned as if they'd choreographed it. Mitch didn't even blink. All he did was lift one hand in a little wave.

Even that made her hot.

He was laid back. God, she loved that.

She needed that.

Not that she needed *him*. Or wanted him. Not like that. She didn't want a man. Not long term for leaning on or anything like that. She shuddered. She was twenty-two, for God's sake. In spite of the fact that her mother and grandmother were convinced she was going to never love anyone the way she loved cats—a fact she hadn't disputed—she had time.

But she *appreciated* spending time with laid-back people. And if those people also said deliciously dirty things, and *did* deliciously dirty things, to her while also making her laugh, then... yeah, that was good. Really good.

Before he headed out the door and got back on the road with his truck pointed south. Very far south. Out of reach and out of you-should-bring-him-to-family-dinner-on-Sunday range.

She couldn't help but smile as everyone turned back to face her, their eyebrows up, a mix of questioning and curiosity and *oh, good for you.* That mostly came from Piper and Max—the big, burly gay man who looked the exact opposite of anyone you would see in a yoga class but who had *amazing* core control and balance.

Yeah, Mitch Landry was something to look at.

Hot. That was just the best word. Hot. Rugged. He clearly worked outside and was completely comfortable in worn denim and t-shirts that molded to his lean, hard, muscled body that could do things that she hadn't ever had done to her before.

He was older than her. Twenty-seven to her twenty-two. And his, ahem, experience showed. She also appreciated that. Along with his laid-back-ness.

She knew more about his sexual skills, of course, since 90 percent of the time they'd been together they'd been naked and doing a lot more than talking.

But when he'd asked for her number and she'd told him that she wasn't looking for anything serious he'd said, "*That* mouth, those eggs, and you don't want any strings attached? I take back everything I've said about the perfect woman not existing."

Yes, he'd complimented both her mouth—and the blow jobs it had given him—and the eggs she'd made him the next morning. Well, at 4 a.m. when they'd finally taken a break and realized they were hungry. He'd added a shit ton of hot sauce to his, but he'd said that had nothing to do with the eggs and everything to do with the fact that his Cajun roots had ruined his taste buds for anything less than a six on a zero-to-ten heat scale.

Then he'd looked her up and down and said that was why when he'd seen the blond who was a ten out of ten on the hot scale he'd had to have her.

It was corny and predictable. But even as she'd rolled her eyes, she'd laughed and maybe even blushed a little. Mostly because yeah, he'd *had her*.

"So looks like the guy is here to check... your heating system," Piper said, stepping forward onto Paige's mat and putting her hands on her shoulders, making Paige focus on Piper's face. "I'll finish the class for you so you can go talk to him."

"Oh, um..." The guy and her heating system...

"He's not from here," someone in the class said.

"I want to get his card though," someone else—someone *female*—said.

That snapped Paige out of her stupor.

Shit. She couldn't have Appleby-ites standing around gawking at Mitch and wondering what he was doing here.

What *was* he doing here? He wasn't supposed to be here for two more days. And it was still early. Or, at least, it wasn't past closing time which was when he was supposed to come by. So she needed to hide him.

She headed for him. "Right. Yes. Mr. Landry. Thanks for coming on short notice. The heating..."

She got close to him, and those green eyes actually twinkled at her. *Twinkled*. Just like the twinkling lights in the big front window in the lobby behind him. His grin grew too. And then she was close enough to feel him. Not with her hands. She didn't reach out and grab him, though she was *itching* to. But she could just *feel* the electricity in the air as she got close. The heat. The chemistry. The magnetism that seemed to pull her body toward his.

He straightened away from the doorframe, his six feet and four inches towering over her. She wasn't as short as her sister or mom, but she needed heels to get to five seven. And she hated heels.

God, he was big. She remembered the way he could lift her and shift her, the way he could position her body *just right*. The way he could...

"The heating?" he asked.

She licked her lips. Right. She'd been talking. About something. "The heating... thing"—Fuck, what did you call the thing that heated a building—"is in here."

She grabbed his sleeve, wanting, *needing* to touch him, and pulled him with her into her office. It was a tiny space behind the front desk. She didn't really need an office except as a place to put stuff. Extra mats and foam rolls and... okay, it was more of a storage room. She did most of her bookwork on her computer while on her couch upstairs in her apartment.

She tugged him inside and shut the door behind them. The furnace... fuck, *furnace*, she hadn't been able to come up with the word *furnace?*... was not in here, but she was hopeful that the people in her class didn't know that or hadn't seen where they'd gone for sure.

"Mitch, I..."

He was right there, all of a sudden, his big body caging her in against the door, his forearms braced on either side of her head, his heat, his scent, his just-being-*him* right there. Finally. After all these months. And, well... to hell with it.

She lifted on tiptoe, put her hand at the back of his neck, and kissed him.

He gave a deep growl and returned the kiss.

And. Then. Some.

Two

S ix months. He'd been without soft lips, soft curves, soft skin for six months. Because the only lips, curves, and skin he wanted had been in Iowa.

Of all places.

Mitch pressed Paige against the door behind her, gripping her hips, and kissing her deeply.

God, he'd thought about her every single day since he'd met her last July. Her bright, sparkling blue eyes, her silky blond hair, her sweet breasts and ass, her sassy mouth, the way she kissed him and touched him like she couldn't get enough either, the way she returned his dirty talk and her humor.

She was perfect. Fucking perfect.

Even though she lived one thousand and forty-two miles away from him.

Which just made her all the *more* perfect. Okay, a few less miles would have been good so they could have met up before six months had passed, but there had been no worries about bumping into her downtown after their hot night together, that was for sure. There'd been no chance that his grandma, Ellie, would return her bra to *her* grandma after Ellie borrowed his truck and found it tucked between the seats.

Yeah, that had happened once.

There'd been no chance of Paige bringing him a pie the next day and sitting on his porch waiting for him to get home. For two hours. And then him showing up with another girl.

That had also happened once. Or twice. The second time the woman had brought brownies, not pie. But still.

Those things wouldn't happen with Paige though. Mostly because he hadn't had even a flicker of interest in another girl since setting eyes on Paige Asher.

But also because Paige wasn't a bake-a-pie-from-scratch-and-show-up-at-a-guy's-house kind of girl. Or brownies. At least, not ones that didn't have zucchini and almond flour in them. She'd only had vegetables and yogurt in her house the next morning when he'd gotten up. No sugar. Not even syrup for the pancakes he'd offered to make. She also hadn't had any regular flour.

She'd also been pretty fine with him getting right on the road and out of town, sans pancakes. So, no, he did not think she'd show up at his house with pie. And she definitely wouldn't wait two hours on his porch swing for him.

Though she might throw the pie in his face when she saw him with another girl the very next night. That's what Abby had done, and he couldn't say he blamed her.

Paige moaned into his mouth, and her fingers slid into his hair, gripping his head and stroking her tongue against his hungrily.

Mitch slid his hands to her ass, clad in the yoga pants that molded to those curves and made him certain that yoga should be a spectator sport, and lifted her.

Her legs wrapped around his waist and he leaned in, pressing her between the door and his hard-as-wood cock. She gasped as he ground into her, wiggling her hips in response, rubbing against him wantonly.

He could easily hold her petite frame with one hand and the press of his body, so he slid a hand up under the short sweatshirt she wore.

This damned thing drove him crazy. Was it coincidence she was wearing the same shirt she'd had on in the kitchen when he'd left her spent and panting on her kitchen table in July? Maybe. Maybe she had a dozen of them. Or maybe it was fate.

She'd come into the kitchen that morning when he'd been rifling through her cupboards, trying to pull together breakfast, in yoga pants and that sweatshirt falling off one shoulder and showing flashes of the smooth skin of her stomach and low back as she moved.

He'd picked her up and pulled that sweatshirt down, sucking on her nipples, making her writhe against him almost instantly, before laying her back on the kitchen table and fucking her thoroughly.

She'd come hard, twice, before his ride pulled up at the curb.

Best. Breakfast. He'd. Ever. Had.

Now he slid his hand up to cup her breast, finding the nipple hard behind the sports bra she wore. She moaned as he plucked at it. She had fantastic nipples. Gorgeous. Sensitive. Playing with them made her pussy clench in the most delicious way.

He pulled the front of the bra down, needing bare skin. The position didn't give him a really good look, but he could feel that soft mound and the sweet, hard tip. He squeezed her nipple as he kissed her and felt her knees tighten around his waist and her press against him more insistently.

"Mitch," she rasped as he dragged his mouth from hers to kiss his way along her jaw to her ear.

"I need to be inside you. I want to talk and catch up too, I swear, but I need to feel you."

"God." She gave a soft half laugh, half moan. "Yes."

"Here? Now?" He'd take her wherever she'd let him have her. But he was aware they were just a few feet and a couple of thin walls away from her yoga studio.

"I want to say yes," she said, letting her head fall back against the door as he kissed down to her neck and then licked the satiny, sweet-smelling skin.

"So say yes."

"I have... people."

He grinned against her collarbone as he rolled her nipple and squeezed her ass. She hadn't been able to come up with the word "furnace" earlier either.

"Those people can find the door," he told her.

He didn't care if she stopped long enough to get rid of every-one. He got it. He wasn't a *complete* Neanderthal. But he also didn't really do a lot of customer service or making-nice in his job. He worked for his cousins and grandparents and was pretty behind the scenes. His cousins ran a swamp boat tour company, Boys of the Bayou, down on the bayou in Louisiana. He did general repairs and cleanup and odd jobs on the buildings and boats and other vehicles they needed for the business. His grand-parents ran the local bar and he did the same for them. Basically he was the go-to guy for anything nonspecific that came up for either business and he just took care of it. No matter what it was. He loved it. He was behind the scenes, had a flexible schedule, was valuable to his family's businesses, but also the businesses weren't going to fold if he wasn't there. It was nearly perfect.

"I need to..." Paige started, but then he shifted her, hoisting her higher and put his mouth on her nipple. "Oh. My. God." The words came out on a soft breath and she arched closer to him.

He knew she was hot and wet now, and he could easily slide inside her sweet body and take them both to the peak within a matter of minutes. If he didn't move his mouth down to her clit and make her come before he fucked her.

They'd only had one night together but they'd covered a lot of bases. He knew her body pretty well and, because she was *so* willing to tell him exactly what she liked, he had a good feel for how to wring every drop of pleasure out of her tight, wonderfully flexible body.

"If you stay in here with me, I'll let you sit on my face," he said against her nipple.

She loved oral sex, but she liked to be on top, controlling the angle and the pace and telling him what to do while she held her pussy above his mouth.

God that had been hot. He'd been *very* willing to follow her directions.

She gave another little groan-laugh. "Suddenly I don't even remember why I thought I should leave this room. Ever."

"That's my girl." He sucked hard on her nipple, ignoring how great it sounded to call her his girl. That was stupid.

Just then the doorknob rattled, and the door shook slightly as someone tried to open it.

"Paige?" a woman's voice called.

Mitch's head came up and he met Paige's eyes. She put a finger to her mouth.

He glanced at the doorknob that rattled again. There was no lock on that knob. The only thing keeping the door shut was their body weight against it.

He pulled Paige's bra back up over her breast, with a touch of regret at having to cover it up, then straightened her shirt.

"Paige Elizabeth! What is going on?"

Paige took a breath and called. "Just a second, Mom!"

Mom? *Mom?* Well, shit.

Paige wiggled against him and he let her slide to the floor. She licked her lips and smoothed her clothes as she pushed him back.

"Are you all right?" the woman asked through the door. "What is going on?"

"I'm just... rearranging the office. I've got the desk in front of the door!" Paige told her. She was frowning and sounded annoyed.

Yeah, he was annoyed too—and very uncomfortable behind his zipper. Mitch adjusted himself and then noticed the doorknob turning.

He quickly moved, leaning into the door, playing the part of a desk, preventing Paige's mom from opening the door.

Paige rolled her eyes. Then she crossed to her desk and shoved it across the floor a few inches, making the scraping noise that her mom would surely hear.

"I'm coming!" she told her mother. She faced Mitch and pointed at him, mouthing. "Hide."

He widened his eyes and shrugged, silently asking, *Where?*

She pointed behind him and he looked over his shoulder. There was a closet. A very small closet. He looked back at her, one eyebrow up. He was a big guy. All over. Something she'd not only enjoyed physically but that she'd commented on more than once when they'd been together. He'd inherited his six-four and wide frame, but he also did manual labor for a living. Working on the bayou just kind of naturally lent itself to brawn.

"Paige!" her mother snapped through the door again.

Paige came close and whispered, "Look, if you don't want to have to propose to me at family dinner on Sunday and have a spring wedding and have constant discussions about which family name we should use for our first child's middle name between now and then, you'll get your cute ass in that closet and stay quiet."

Proposals, Sunday family dinner, wedding planning and family names used as middle names... all of that was *way* too familiar. He knew exactly what she was talking about suddenly.

He was going to learn more about her family once they were alone—seemed they had something in common besides burn-the-bed-up sex—but yeah, for now, he could hide out.

He gave her a nod and turned for the closet and slipped inside. Barely. It was definitely a tight fit.

The tiny space was filled with hoodies and coats, a couple pairs of boots on the floor, and a shovel—he assumed for the snow outside, which, he couldn't deny, made him grin. He'd never spent time in a place that got regular snow and that was going to be fun.

The door had barely closed behind him when he heard Paige open the office door.

"Good heavens!" her mother said. "I was starting to get worried."

"I'm fine. I was looking for some... files... and got to rearranging and had the desk in front of the door," Paige said.

"You look flushed. Are you feeling okay?" her mom asked.

Mitch grinned. She did look flushed. But she was feeling just fine. Well, horny, he'd bet. But not sick.

"I'm *fine*," Paige said, sounding exasperated. "What are you doing here?"

"Why aren't you doing your class?" Mrs. Asher asked.

"Because I had something to take care of in here."

Again, Mitch grinned.

"Shouldn't you take care of your business things and files and rearranging between classes?" her mother asked. "You don't have *that* many classes to start with."

Mitch could hear Paige's sigh even through the closed closet door.

"Mom, I'm handling my business just fine."

"But if you have to pay someone else to lead a class, then it's less money—"

"*Mom*, it's fine!" Paige snapped. "What are you doing here?"

Now Mitch heard her mother's sigh. The dramatic sighing was genetic. Yeah, he could understand that too. He also had very passionate women in his family.

"Your sister said that you had a headache last night and couldn't come over and help the kids with their projects. So I brought you some medicine."

There was a long pause. So long that Mitch thought maybe they'd moved out of the office into the outer lobby and he just couldn't hear them talking any longer.

But a moment later, Paige said, "You mean, you came over here to find out why I wouldn't go help Amanda's kids with their festival projects because you don't believe I had a headache. But you passive-aggressively brought me medicine to pretend to be concerned."

Mitch could have sworn she was talking through gritted teeth.

"Paige, I would never do that," Mrs. Asher said. "I was concerned. You rarely have headaches."

"That's true," Paige said. "Because I'm very good at taking care of my body, and if I *do* have a pain or ache, I have many ways of taking care of it."

"Oils and herbs," her mother said.

Mitch could practically hear the eye roll that accompanied that comment.

"Yes," Paige said. "Oils and herbs. And trigger-point work. And meditation. And rest. None of which I could have at Amanda's house."

"Well, I brought you this in case none of that worked."

"You know I'm not going to use this," Paige told her.

"You don't have to admit it. I won't ask. But you have it just in case you need it. It's your own little secret."

"If I *did* use ibuprofen secretly, don't you think that I would be able to get it myself?" Paige asked.

"Where would you get it? You wouldn't want anyone in town to know that you were using a real medicine."

"First, the things I use to deal with aches and pains *are* just as real as this," Paige said. "And secondly, I'm not trying to say that ibuprofen doesn't work, Mother. I don't judge people who use it. If I needed it and wanted to use it, I'd go buy it at the store."

"You wouldn't," her mother said. "You want people to believe that what you do is the best choice."

"It's the best choice *for me*."

"So you wouldn't go buy ibuprofen at the store."

"Because I don't use ibuprofen. Not because I'm trying to trick people into thinking that what I do works when really I'm using over-the-counter painkillers secretly."

Mitch had to squeeze his hand into a fist to keep from bursting through the door and interrupting. Paige's mother was annoying her and he wanted to intervene.

Which was absolutely ridiculous. He barely knew her, and he

sincerely doubted that she needed his help. Plus it was her *mother*. That was not the right first impression to make. Probably.

It was possibly because her mother was meddling and he knew a lot about that. Meddling in the Landry family was like game night in other families. Something they all got together to do on a regular basis.

"How's your head today?" Paige's mother asked.

"Fine."

"So you could help your niece and nephew with their projects tonight?"

"No. I have plans tonight."

"Doing what?"

"Mom, we've talked about this. You don't need to know every single thing I do."

"So it's a boy."

"I'm twenty-two. I don't date boys."

"But it is a date?"

"No, it's not a date."

Mitch grinned. So wild, up-all-night sex wasn't a date in her book? He could live with that. He was hoping for some snow time though, he wouldn't lie. Snow was a novelty to a guy born and raised in Louisiana. He'd seen it twice and it had lasted for about two hours each time. It had been years. When Tori, his cousin's fiancé and the Iowa girl who had introduced him to Paige in the first place, had been preparing him for this trip north in January, she'd talked about boots and coats and gloves and when she'd told him that Appleby had about six inches of snow on the ground currently he'd admit that he'd felt a definite boyish rush of excitement. Maybe he could talk Paige into making a snowman or sledding or ice skating. He had no fucking idea how to ice skate, but he felt that was very winter wonder-land-ish and that he might regret returning south without having at least *tried*.

And hot chocolate. He really wanted hot chocolate.

"But it involves a b—man?" Mrs. Asher asked.

"Mom, I said I have plans. I can't help with an art project. That's all you need to know."

"I just care."

"You're just nosy."

"I just think you could help your sister out once in a while."

"I just think my sister could have figured out how to use her birth control before she had little people she needed help with."

"Paige Elizabeth!" her mother gasped.

"You act like that's the first time I've said that," Paige said. Her tone was exasperated but also held a hint of amusement.

Mitch wished he could see her face.

"I'm always shocked when you say things like that," her mother said, definitely sounding shocked. "I keep thinking that you're going to get over this anti-marriage and family thing you have going on."

"Maybe. But I wouldn't hold your breath."

She was anti-marriage and family? Mitch felt his eyebrows rise. A part of him liked that. All the women he knew back home were very pro-marriage and family. He was twenty-seven. The girls on the bayou had been trying to tie him down—or their mamas had, at least—for five years now.

His own family had laid off on that for the most part. Or the attention had been focused on his older cousins. Until recently. His cousins had all spent the past summer falling ass over boots in love. Even his new buddy, Chase, who spent most of his time in medical school at Georgetown, had found himself smitten, somehow. Mitch had really thought Chase would be immune. They'd had a hell of a good time partying together. But Bailey Wilcox had happened and Chase was now a goner too.

Now the attention had shifted to Mitch. No one had yet said anything like, *when are you going to settle down?* But if they knew he was up here visiting a woman he'd met in July and hadn't been able to stop thinking about, they'd all be *very* interested.

There were three things the Landrys believed in with their whole hearts. One, crawfish boils were the way to fix any rift, disappointment or broken heart. Two, everyone's business was everyone else's business. And three, falling in love was the ultimate goal in life... even if you had to do it a few times to get it right.

Mitch couldn't help but wonder what his family would think of Paige. She was a yoga-doing-meditating vegetarian who clearly liked to keep her personal business personal. None of that would make sense to them.

And the Landrys would, most likely, horrify Paige.

He grinned thinking of it. His family was loud, and their idea of meditation was sitting in a boat and fishing without talking for twenty minutes straight. Other than swearing at the fish, and the fishing line, and the tree branches hidden under the surface of the water that messed with those lines.

He'd known Paige was a fling-with-no-strings girl. He'd texted her first and it had taken a couple of days for her to respond. He'd given up on hearing back from her by the time his phone had dinged with the message from her. The message that read *I can't believe you texted me.*

He'd laughed and texted back—right away, incidentally, which might have been a mistake—and said, *why can't you believe it?*

Because I'm not sending you naked photos.

I don't need photos. I got a very good look at <u>everything</u> and I have a VERY good memory.

It had taken a few minutes after that and he'd wondered if he'd screwed up but then she'd replied, *so what do you want?*

And he'd had to really think about that.

Clearly, she hadn't been thrilled to hear from him. She hadn't been waiting with bated breath to see if he'd text or call. She hadn't been flirtatious or encouraging in keeping the conversation going.

At first.

But as long as he was okay with twelve to twenty-four hours

passing between messages from her, he did hear from her, and every damned time she made him smile.

He'd ask stupid shit like, *what did you do today?*

And she'd say, *scooped cat poop, did yoga, rinse, repeat.*

He hadn't been able to resist asking, *what about a shower? You probably took a shower right?*

She'd reply, eventually, *I did.*

That was it. Nothing flirtatious or dirty.

Until about three weeks in when, in answer to his question about what she did that day, she texted, *scooped cat poop, did yoga, got off with my vibrator while thinking of you, rinse, repeat.*

He'd almost swallowed his tongue. He'd typed three messages before finally sending, *please tell me the repeat was with the vibrator and thinking of me too.*

Her reply, *Definitely. Twice last night. Once this morning, Once just now.*

She'd texted him *right after* using her vibrator and thinking of him.

Now *that* was what he was talking about.

Strangely, from there, their conversations had gotten more in depth. She'd told him more about her cats and why she loved yoga and she'd even drunk texted him after a girls' night, and, instead of getting dirtier, she'd told him that she wished they'd had more time together and that she'd made vegetarian gumbo. Which wasn't really gumbo at all—how could it be without shrimp or sausage or at least chicken?—but he'd been stupidly touched that she'd tried something from his world and he hadn't had the heart to tell her it didn't count.

He'd told her about the bayou and what he loved about it, how he loved the outdoors, and about his family. Which now, listening to her and her mother, he realized might have been a mistake.

He came from a very big, very nosy, very involved family. If she had too much of that here, she would have very little desire to meet his intrusive relatives.

But why was he thinking about her meeting his family?

That wasn't going to happen. That was the beauty of this situation. She lived *far* away. To see her, it took him miles away from the bayou and his family, and their time together would always be temporary. It would be impossible to get serious. Even if either of them were interested in that at all. Which they clearly weren't.

Suddenly the closet door opened and Paige stood there.

He must have missed her mom leaving.

"Sorry about that."

"No problem."

She grimaced. "I'm not so sure about that."

He reached for her. "I have lots of other things for your mouth to do rather than apologize."

But she backed up before he could catch ahold of her.

"And while I would *very much* like to use my mouth in *all* of those ways and few others, we need to cool it for a little bit."

He frowned, stepping out of the closet. "What do you mean?"

"I mean, there are going to be other family members stopping by over the next few hours."

"There will be?"

"Oh, for sure." She paced away from him. "Mom's suspicious now, and I kind of admitted, stupidly, that my plans tonight involve a guy." She turned back to face him from several feet away. She was frowning. "That was really careless of me, of course. But I blame you."

"Me?"

"You scrambled my brain and then you were just *right in there*."

"I was totally quiet," he protested around a grin about her scrambled-brain confession.

"Yeah, but you were *there*. Just a few feet away. Being all hot and stuff."

"I was being hot? From inside a closet? With the door

closed?" He liked that a lot. And knew what she meant, actually. He'd been very aware of her just on the other side of the door as well.

"Yeah." She shook her head. "It must be the testosterone. You've got so much oozing out all over that it got on the floor and seeped out from under the door and soaked into me."

He laughed softly and crossed the space between them. He reached out before she could move back and caught her wrist, bringing her up against him. He bent to put his face against her neck, breathing deeply of her scent and loving the feel of her hair against his cheek and the way she shivered in his arms.

"The oozing doesn't sound particularly sexy, but I love the idea of soaking into you," he said, gruffly against her ear. "Does it make you hot?"

She sighed. "Yes."

"So you were distracted because your panties are wet, and your pussy is aching knowing that the cock you want more than anything is just a few feet away and is all ready for you."

She shivered again, and her arms went around him as she arched closer. "Yes."

"You want my cock so much you couldn't even come up with a lie for your mama?"

She huffed a soft laugh. "I guess."

"So we just have to hide out while these people stop by. We'll keep the lights off, and I'll just flip you on your stomach while I'm fucking you so you can scream into the pillow."

Paige gave a lusty sigh and then shook her head. "Won't work unless we hide my car. And change the locks."

He pulled back. "They have keys?"

"A few of them. My two sisters do. And one of my friends. She won't give it up though."

"Your sisters might?"

"You don't understand my mother's powers."

Actually, he kind of did. In his case, it was his grandmother, but he understood how manipulative a matriarch could be when she really put her mind to it.

"So what's the solution?"

"I answer the door each time and convince them that nothing is going on and that I was making the guy up and that I'm just a bitch who doesn't want to do art projects with her niece and nephew."

He squinted at her.

She laughed. "You're nice not to ask it out loud, but, yes, they will be able to believe that."

"Your family will believe that you're willing to lie to get out of family activities?"

She shrugged. "They think the fact that I like cats better than people is a huge character flaw and they mourn my lack of maternal instinct. They also think that I'm selfish when I don't want to be Super Aunt. Especially because my other sister Josie *is* a super aunt. And she's completely into romance and marriage and family. It took her until age twenty-five to find Mr. Perfect, but she was always hopeful and open to it. So they never gave her any crap about being single and nearing spinster age." Paige rolled her eyes. "They secretly hope that if I spend time around my sister's kids that it will flip the biological clock switch in me, but the truth is, I'm not that into kids. Even ones I'm related to."

He was from a family where everyone helped raise all the kids, and the kids were as close to their aunts and uncles and grandparents as they were to their own parents. In his case, he was *closer* to his relatives than to his mom and dad. His dad had been a single dad and had happily accepted the help offered from his extended family. Mitch had been an only child but had essentially grown up with a huge family with cousins that felt more like siblings.

His Aunt Hannah had absolutely been like a mother with plenty of influence from his grandmother, her best friend, and his other aunts as well.

He had to admit, as much as he related to Paige not enjoying the nosiness of her family, he didn't really understand her not wanting to be involved in their lives, at least to an extent.

But it didn't matter. He didn't need to know how Paige Asher felt about kids. He needed to know how she felt about incorporating flavored body lotion into foreplay. At most.

"So how's this going to go?" he asked, focusing on her breasts and hips and the fact that it was awesome that she wasn't looking at him as potential marriage material.

She rolled her eyes. "Various people will need to borrow something or drop something off, or they'll claim I wasn't answering my phone, and they *had* to know how I felt about something. So we can hang out and *make out*," she said with a mischievous smile. "But I'll have to stay somewhat dressed, and we won't be able to get *totally* into it until my grandpa comes and goes."

"Your grandpa?"

She nodded. "He's always the last one. Because he's the one I have the hardest time saying no to. Because he's actually sweet and sincerely concerned about me. But once he leaves, we should be good."

"So..." Mitch settled his hands on her hips and brought her close again. "Kind of like the ghosts in *A Christmas Carol.*"

She looked surprised, then laughed. "How so?"

"Visitors over the course of the evening trying to teach you something."

She laughed again. "Trying to teach me what exactly?"

"About keeping secrets from your family?"

"Maybe."

"That they care and just want to be sure you're okay?"

She narrowed her eyes and shook her head. "Nope. You can't get soft. If you start to side with them, you're sleeping at Tori's tonight."

He wasn't worried. He knew she wanted him in her bed. He shook his head. "Can't. They dropped me off and left me. I'd have to hitchhike. And I don't have a winter coat," he added with a grin. "I'd freeze my nuts off. And you like my nuts."

"I might like them less if you start to sympathize with my busybody relatives."

He pressed said nuts—more or less—against her. "Nah. You're addicted."

"I've gone without them for six months."

"Ridiculous to go without them any longer," he said with a nod. "I promise not to say nice things about your family as long as you have your mouth or pussy against those nuts."

Her eyes flared with heat. "Hmm... you drive a hard bargain."

He pressed his cock against her. "Very hard." He couldn't pass that pun up.

She licked her lips and he swore that he got even harder. If that were possible.

"So you're up for this?" she asked, emphasizing *up*.

"What I heard you describe was *lots* of foreplay and creativity with prolonged release," he said. He dropped his voice. "Basically it means that you're going to be hot and dripping and desperate by the time you shut and lock that door for the last time. *That* sounds like a fucking fantastic belated Christmas present with a big old red bow around it, sweetheart."

She just looked at him for a long moment.

Sweetheart hung in the air between them.

He wondered if she'd call him on it. She didn't seem like the type to like endearments. She wasn't soft and sweet and romantic. She was sassy and sexy and fun.

And that's what he wanted.

Never mind that he had a package of the pancake mix his grandmother's best friend used in their restaurant in his bag. Just in case Paige would let him make her breakfast in the morning.

"Fine," she finally said, her voice a little husky. "Then you can stay and help me... kill time... in between visitors."

"It will be my pleasure."

Three

She was playing with fire. And it was so much fun.

Paige was grinning as she stepped in front of the mirror that hung in her office and straightened her clothes and ran her fingers through her hair.

Mitch was here.

It was going to be a pain now that her mother had smelled a secret, but it was also going to be fun. He hadn't batted an eye at the idea of multiple relatives stopping by and repeatedly interrupting their naked plans.

Prolonged foreplay sounded pretty great. Frustrating, of course. But great.

They definitely hadn't done it that way the first time. They'd pretty much made some stupid excuse why they both had to leave the alpaca farm at the same time—yes, they'd met at an alpaca farm—and had barely gotten through her apartment door before they'd ripped each other's clothes off. They'd been fucking up against her door within five minutes. She hadn't *needed* any foreplay. She'd been so, so ready for him.

That had been wild. She'd never wanted a guy that much that quickly.

In spite of the fact they'd met over the back of an alpaca.

Her friend and veterinarian, Tori, had come back to Iowa to gather her menagerie of special-needs animals she'd been collecting to relocate them to Louisiana with her back in March. Her boyfriend, Josh, and his cousin Mitch had come along to help. It wasn't a small feat to move cows and pigs and a passel of cats and dogs a thousand miles to a new home.

But it wasn't until Tori had come back to visit her parents in July—and to take another few goats and another cow back with her—that Paige had met them. She'd simply gone out to Tori's place to say hi. She hadn't expected to get the hottest one-night stand of her life out of it. But she'd been more than happy with how the visit had turned out.

And now he was back. To see her. Tori didn't need his help this time. Yes, she was taking an alpaca back to Louisiana with her, but she and Josh could handle one animal. Mitch was here to see Paige. And that made her belly flutter and her chest feel warmer than it should have.

She shook that off. She needed to just focus. On getting Mitch out of here and up to her apartment before anyone planned a bridal shower and then getting him naked as soon as possible.

"Okay, we'll go out together and pretend to be talking about the heating system," she told him.

"Furnace," he told her with a grin. "It's called a furnace."

She swatted his arm. "Yeah. Okay. The furnace." So he knew that she'd lost her ability to think of the word furnace. It was okay he knew that he affected her. He did. And what would hiding that get her?

"So we're going to talk about the work I did on your furnace?" he asked, somehow making the question sound dirty.

She laughed. "Yes."

"Without any tools?" he asked, turning his empty palms up.

She shrugged. "There might not be anyone outside anyway. But I guess we can talk about the work you're *going to do?*"

He wiggled his brows. "I definitely have a lot of thoughts about what I'm going to do to your heating system."

It was the drawl. It had to be. How did that cheesy teasing make her stomach flip and her want to giggle? It was the most obvious line he could have used. *Any* other guy probably would have said the same thing. But Mitch Landry said it and her libido started dancing to "Single Ladies." And singing.

NO. No, no, no.

He was *not* going to put a ring on it.

"Yeah, so…" She cleared her throat. "Say something about…"

"Nuts?" he offered. "Or screws, maybe? I could talk about things I need to bang. Or pound. Or what a tight fit it will be."

She put her hand over his mouth, shaking her head, telling her libido to knock it off. "How about you make something up about a duct or something?"

She felt him grin behind her hand. His fingers wrapped around her wrist and he pulled her hand back. But not before kissing her palm and sending tiny electric shocks to her belly.

"I can do that," he said.

"Okay, great." Her voice was breathless. Maybe even more so than when he'd had her pinned against the door. What was that?

She didn't want to analyze it.

She took a breath and turned toward the door.

"I really think it's your blower motor," Mitch said from behind her.

She started to snort as she stepped out into the lobby.

And into a small crowd of women.

She came up short, surprised. "Uh, hi, ladies."

There were only three women left over from the earlier class, but the way they'd all swung toward the door and had wide eyes and expectant looks on their faces made them seem more numerous somehow.

Paige felt Mitch stop directly behind her. Not quite bumping into her but not with any real *space* between them.

Her blower motor. Uh-huh.

"I was hoping you could take a look at my furnace too," Linda Ritter said.

To Mitch.

Her gaze had slid right past Paige to the man over her shoulder.

"Oh," he said. "Well... yes."

Paige frowned and turned to face him. "You don't have to do that."

"He's a repairman, right?" Linda asked.

"He's just..."

"Passing through," Mitch supplied.

"But you're looking at Paige's blower motor?" Linda asked. "How long will that take?"

Mitch cleared his throat and Paige knew he was *not* thinking about her furnace. She wanted to elbow him but that would have been very obvious to their little audience here.

"I probably won't be available for anything else until tomorrow," he said.

He sounded as if he actually meant to take a look at Linda's furnace. And Linda was fifty-something, happily married, with four kids, and was a first-grade teacher. Paige thought she *actually* wanted Mitch to *actually* look at her *actual* furnace.

"Tomorrow is fine," Linda said. "We've been at my mom's for the past two days. One more night will be okay. We'd just be so grateful."

Paige frowned and focused on Linda. "Your furnace has been out for two days?"

She nodded. "And with the big storm this week, Larry and Mike have been swamped with work on a couple of roofs that had tree branches come down, so they can't get over to look at furnaces."

This was not good. Linda didn't just need her furnace filters cleaned out or something. She actually needed it repaired. And now, because of her lie about who Mitch was, Linda was going to have the hopes that she'd be back in her own warm home tomorrow night.

"Oh wow, if you're completely without heat, I'll stop by this afternoon," Mitch said.

Paige turned back to him again. She was going to have whiplash. She frowned at him. He just lifted a brow at her.

Did he actually know how to fix furnaces? Huh. That hadn't occurred to her.

"Do you know anything about gas fireplaces?" Melanie Carter asked.

Paige tipped her head, curious about the answer too.

He nodded. "I could take a look."

Paige widened her eyes at him. He widened his eyes back at her.

Damn, he knew about furnaces and fireplaces. That was… lucky. Or something.

Like hot. And not in the those-were-both-ways-people-heated-their-homes way. It was sexy that he knew how to fix things. And that he was willing to go help complete strangers like that.

"Are you in town for a few days?" Carol Lemming asked Mitch.

He nodded. "I am. I'm passing through, meeting up with some friends in a couple of days, but heard there was a great festival here and thought I might stay for a day or two."

"How did you know he works on furnaces?" Melanie asked Paige.

"Um…" Paige was distracted by the *day or two* thing. She'd thought this was a one-night thing again, like last time.

She was going to have to hide him for a day or two?

Except now he was going to be going out all over town fixing things.

Okay, he was going to go to *two* houses and help a couple of people out. But now all of these ladies knew he was here, *for a day or two.*

33

Her mom was so going to hear about this.

She was absolutely going to have to be *sure* her mother thought that Mitch was *just* a friend of a friend who had taken a look at her blower motor.

In a very not dirty way.

"The friends I'm meeting are mutual friends," Mitch said, when Paige had failed to answer Melanie for too long. "They mentioned that she'd been having some issues here at the studio and I offered to stop by on my way through."

"You're so sweet."

"That's so fortunate for you, Paige."

"Are you single?"

The three responses came right on top of one another, and the question about his relationship status was almost lost.

Almost.

"He's engaged," she said, before she really thought it through.

It was a great excuse for her mother *not* to think Paige should spend romantic time with Mitch for the *day or two*—why had he not mentioned that?—he was going to be in town.

Mitch gave a little choked sound behind her, but Paige covered it by saying brightly, "To Tori Kramer. Do you ladies know her? Veterinarian?"

But that made Mitch choke and cough again.

"Tori and I have been friends for a while," Paige went on, talking quickly so that no one, including Mitch, could insert anything until she'd laid the whole story out.

"She went to Mardi Gras last year and met J—Mitch, and they kind of fell for each other, but she came back to Iowa, and they made a deal to meet up at Mardi Gras again this year if they were still interested in one another. She was, but she also happened to be down there for her best friend's wedding, and she went to find Jo—*Mitch*, she went to find Mitch again, and all the old feelings were still there and bam, they fell in love and now she's moving down there to be with him."

Paige finished the actually true story about Tori—it just

happened that the guy in the story was Mitch's cousin Josh—with a bright smile. "So Mitch is just here, in Appleby, to help with my furnace because Tori told him it went out."

"Oh, how nice," Melanie said. But she sounded disappointed.

Paige frowned at that as well. Melanie was also married but had only been with her husband for a couple of years. Surely she wasn't looking for a hookup with a hot repairman? Well, stranger things had happened.

"It doesn't feel cold in here," Carol commented.

Right. The building was warm. Which was strange if the furnace was out. "Well—"

"It's not *out*," Mitch interjected. "Not exactly. The blower motor just isn't working efficiently. So the furnace is on, but the air isn't circulating as well as it should be."

Wait a second... the blower motor was a real thing? And here she'd been thinking that was a pretty great innuendo.

"So you're staying with your fiancé tonight, then?" Carol asked.

Mitch looked down at Paige. "Well, I was thinking maybe I should stick around here and offer some help with all of the trees and roofs."

Paige gaped at him. "Seriously?"

"Tori will understand," he said dryly. Then he shrugged. "Sounds like it's a town-wide issue. I'm not used to snow, but I know how to use a chainsaw."

"I bet you do," Melanie said.

When Paige glanced at her, Melanie's gaze was on Mitch's right bicep.

Stupidly, Paige found herself moving to block Melanie's line of sight. Not that she totally could, of course. Mitch was a big guy—something she *really* liked about him—but she still felt the need to insinuate herself between him and the other woman.

"But you don't have a winter coat," Paige pointed out to Mitch.

"Know anyone who would loan me one?" he asked her with a smirk that said he'd noticed her move between him and Melanie.

"I—"

"Coats and anything else you need," Carol assured him. "I was going to ask you if you knew anything about electrical wiring."

Paige looked at her. Of course they could come up with coats and hats and gloves and anything else. Everyone in town had multiples of all of those things. Carol had three adult sons herself who probably had coats that would fit Mitch. "Why do you need help with electrical wiring?"

"My booth for the festival has a glitch," the woman said, lifting her shoulder.

"But you had no idea Mitch would be here," Paige pointed out. "What was your plan?" Carol was a friend of her mother's. She would absolutely be reporting all of this back to Dee Asher.

"I was going to do without the lights," Carol told her. "Liam hooked it all up for me yesterday, but then he had to head to Dubuque for work," she said of her son. "I hated to call him back when it all went out this morning. I just thought, since Mitch was here and was obviously so capable, that I might as well ask."

Mitch was already nodding. "I can definitely take a look. No problem."

"Well..." Carol said.

Paige bit back a sigh. "There's something else?"

"It's not just my booth. Apparently, the problem is a wider electrical issue for the whole square. None of the booths have electricity."

"And normally Mike and Larry would be fixing it but they're repairing roofs," Paige filled in, letting a tiny sigh out.

"Mike and Larry work for the city. They're the general repairmen," Linda explained to Mitch. "The branches that came down were on trees in an older part of town. The houses are close together, and the four that were damaged all had older roofs."

"*Four?*" Paige interrupted. "Mike and Larry are crawling around on snowy roofs on *four* houses in this cold?"

Linda nodded. "Roof holes obviously take precedence over lights on the festival booths."

"Well, of course," Paige said. She hadn't known there were people with *holes* in their roofs or that Larry, who was easily sixty, and Mike, who wasn't much younger, were up on rooftops that had icicles dangling and snowy patches. "Why aren't they hiring a roofing company?"

"The trees should have been trimmed back before this happened," Carol said. "That was the city's responsibility, so the repairs are too."

"They're risking Mike and Larry's necks to save a few bucks?" Paige asked.

Carol just shrugged.

"The wiring won't take long, I'm bettin'," Mitch said, his drawl slow and easy, making Paige take a long, deep breath.

She felt his fingers brush against her lower back and found the gesture reassuring.

Of course, he was supposed to be engaged, so she shifted away from the touch.

"I'll get the furnace up and going," Mitch said. "I'll take a peek at the fireplace, check the wiring quick, and then go help Mike and Larry."

That was going to really cut into the naked time they could be having, Paige realized. But she'd not realized they were going to have *days* of it.

What was she going to do with him for *a couple of days* anyway? Besides the obvious. But they couldn't just have sex for forty-eight hours straight. Could they? Of course not. She had to work. For one thing. And if he was off doing other things, then it was less time they'd be together and making her mother suspicious. The Tori story was solid. Her mom knew of Tori. Paige had talked about her often enough. Dee had maybe even met Tori once when she'd been here looking at the cats.

Yeah, this wasn't a terrible plan.

"Oh, you need to go do the furnace first and then help Mike

and Larry," Melanie said, waving her hand. "My fireplace can wait. It's not our main heat source."

"And our lights can wait," Carol agreed. "If you can get to it, that's wonderful, but Mike and Larry can use the help."

"Okay, then," Mitch said. "I assume Paige knows where y'all live?"

Paige could tell the drawl affected the other women as well. Their smiles all got a little bigger when he said *y'all*.

"She does, of course," Linda said. "You can stop by any time. If you want to come around dinnertime, I'd—"

"No," Paige cut in on the dinner invitation. For fuck's sake. Linda was going to, what? Adopt him as a pseudo-son? Or had she been eyeing his biceps too? Or was it the drawl?

"No," Paige said again. "Mitch will be fine. He can stop over and look at the furnace tonight and then get in touch with Mike and Larry. Then I'll be sure he's fed tonight."

"And Tori?" Melanie asked. "She'll be okay with sharing you with us?"

"She's with her family tonight," Mitch said. "I was gonna check on Paige's furnace and then head over there, but she'll completely understand if I hang out here and help y'all out."

Blatant lying for her, Paige noted. That should not be sexy. She should not condone lying. Though she had put him in the position to have to. She shouldn't have done that either. She was clearly a bad influence on a man who was turning out to be a really good guy.

This had been a lot easier on her conscience when all she'd known about him was how good he was with his hands and mouth and... other body parts.

"Oh, you'll have to invite Tori over to the festival," Carol said. "And the friends you're meeting up with. Especially after you save the entire thing by fixing the wiring."

Well, *that* was a terrible idea.

Tori would probably love to come. She was now a Louisiana girl, but she'd maybe missed Iowa and the snow and other wintery things her new home didn't offer. But that would mean she'd have to pretend to be Mitch's fiancée. How would Paige get her to do that? And then what would they do with Josh? Make him stay with Tori's family? No. He'd be a hot, single guy in town with Tori and Mitch, and Paige's mother would try to set her up with *him*. That would be more than a little awkward.

"Tori's mom has really missed her," Mitch said smoothly. "As much as she'd love the festival, I'm sure, I think they want to spend every minute together that they can. I don't want her to be even more annoyed with me for stealing her little girl to the South."

A slow, sexy smile accompanied his explanation—that totally fixed the problem *and* kept Paige from having to lie even more—and the other women visibly melted a little.

Paige almost rolled her eyes. Except that she completely understood what they were feeling. The guy was potent. And quick on his feet. And could, apparently, fix just about anything.

Damn, she was in trouble.

"Well, you still be sure to tell her how her man saved the entire Apple Festival," Carol said.

"It's just a few lights," Paige said with a smile. "I mean, saving the entire thing is a little dramatic, isn't it?"

"It's all of the electricity," Carol said. "It's the light and the sound system for the music and the PA system. It's the outlets that will keep the cider and kettle corn warm. It's everything."

Paige stared at her. "You... didn't say that."

"I didn't want Mitch to feel bad if he couldn't fix it."

"But he might not be able to fix it," Paige said.

"Oh, he can," Carol said with conviction and a huge smile at Mitch. "I mean, I didn't know that when I first asked. It was just a hope that if he knew heating, he'd know electrical. But he's clearly very confident."

Paige agreed that he seemed sure of himself but to pin the success of the Apple Festival on him... a stranger... who had stumbled into the situation... and who she would really like to keep naked in her bed while he was in town...

But dammit, Mike and Larry shouldn't be up on those roofs. Not that they weren't able, but it was *cold*. An extra pair of hands —very capable and strong and big hands—would definitely help them out.

She felt a little pinch at the base of her spine. She looked over her shoulder at the pincher.

"It will be fine," Mitch said, meeting her eyes before looking up at the other women. "I might need to borrow some tools, but I can do whatever needs done."

"Tools aren't a problem," Carol said quickly.

"For sure," Linda added. "Someone in this town will have anything you need. More than one someone, I'm sure."

"Great," Mitch said. "Then I'm your man."

"Yeah, you are," Melanie said, not quite under her breath.

Paige frowned at her again. That was so inappropriate. "Okay, so," she said, stepping forward and gesturing toward the front door, "I'll fill Mitch in on the festival, tell him where you live, connect him with my... some tools."

Dammit. She'd almost said her dad. She was *not* going to introduce Mitch to her dad even in order for him to borrow tools. Her family was going to hear about Mitch soon enough, and she was certain the information would include that he'd been recruited at her yoga studio and that he was engaged to a friend of hers.

Fortunately, the word *engaged* would very likely be used and that would save her from having to answer questions about her interest in him.

But there was a niggle in the back of her mind that said she didn't like the idea of having to pretend she had no interest. Or that he was connected to someone else.

A really stupid niggle.

She didn't *want* them to think she was interested. She wasn't *interested*. Not in a let's-pick-out-bathroom-tile-and-maybe-a-couple-of-kids'-names way. And that's what her mom would think "interested" should mean.

The women filed past her out into the chilly afternoon with various versions of "Nice to meet you, Mitch" and "See you later."

She let the door close behind them and turned the lock. She didn't have another class for an hour, and she could do without any more people ambushing them. What had started with a simple secret visit to town for a quickie had suddenly turned into Mitch helping the entire town with fix-it projects. And saving the entire Apple Festival.

She pivoted back and said, "Come on."

She rounded the front desk and pulled open the door that revealed the staircase to the upper floor where she lived.

Paige was aware of his eyes on her ass as she climbed the steps in front of him, but he didn't touch her or say anything until they were both inside her apartment and she had that door shut and locked as well.

"I'm engaged to Tori?" he asked.

That wasn't what she'd been expecting. "It was the first thing to come to mind."

"It's really that big of a deal your mom think there's no chance anything could happen between us?"

"It really is."

He looked at her for a long moment. Then nodded. "Okay."

She blew out a relieved breath. "Really?"

"I get it."

She tipped her head. "You do?"

"I didn't tell my family about the sassy, sexy blond I was coming all the way up here to see."

She smiled softly. "Why not?"

"Because they've already noticed that I haven't been going out as much, and I haven't had a woman at my place since July."

Her eyes were totally round, she was sure, by the time he finished. Oh boy, huge, flashing, cherry-red sign. He hadn't had a woman at his place since they'd met? She had the impression that not having women over on a regular basis was very unusual. She hadn't been with anyone since she'd met him either and that was giving her a very itchy, uncomfortable, uh-oh feeling. But to know it was the same for him...

"You should definitely go look at Linda's furnace," she said. She crossed the room and grabbed her phone off the short breakfast bar between her kitchen and tiny living room.

She glanced up at him as she scrolled through to find her friend Max's phone number.

Mitch was watching her with an unreadable expression. She blew out a breath. "You do actually know how to do all the things you told the women you could do?"

"Yes."

"You're sure you can fix all of it?"

"One hundred percent."

She dropped her arm and regarded him. "What do you do for a living?"

"Whatever my grandma's restaurant and bar, or my cousins' tour company, needs me to do. I can fix anything. Motors, electric, plumbing, brickwork, roofs, drywall. You name it."

Without meaning to, she let her gaze travel over his body. His big, hard, muscled body.

In three seconds he was in front of her, crowding close.

"What are you doing?" she asked breathlessly, feeling her body lean into his instinctively.

"You can't look at me like that without me coming over here and taking you up on what you're offering."

"Was I..." She had to stop and wet her lips. "Was I offering you something?"

"This sweet body spread out on that countertop behind you," he said with a nod.

"I was checking *you* out."

"Yeah and wanting everything you know I can do to you."

Well, that was true.

"I... you... need to go get those repairs done."

"You're throwing me out because I freaked you out."

"I..." She pressed her lips together and nodded. "Yeah."

"I haven't wanted anyone but you since we met."

"Yeah, that's... a little freaky."

"You're sorry I haven't fucked anyone else since you?"

God, when he talked like that how was she supposed to stay on topic? Especially the topic of *not* wanting him to be all hers all the time, and to hell with the fact that she was too damned young to be serious about someone.

"Not sorry," she confessed.

"Me neither."

Her heart kicked in her chest. "You're not falling in love with me," she told him softly.

"That would be ridiculous," he agreed.

"It would." But it really should have felt more ridiculous than it did.

"But," he said, "I don't want to be with anyone else. And I'm afraid I might not get over that."

Another kick against her rib cage. And a shot of fear. Because she felt the same way if she were being totally honest.

"You don't want to move to Iowa," she pointed out.

"I don't mind it so far."

She gave a soft laugh. "Give it time."

"Okay."

She sobered immediately. "Mitch—"

He lowered his head and covered her mouth with his. He kissed her long and deep, cupping her face with one hand and her hip with the other in a sweet, possessive hold.

When he broke the kiss long seconds later, he simply said, "Don't freak out."

Too late.

Four

An impressive fifteen minutes later, Mitch was in a bulky winter coat with a toolbox in hand—thanks to Paige's friend Max—and was walking up the front sidewalk to Linda Ritter's house.

He wasn't even sure how that had all happened. It was like Paige snapped her fingers, and everything she needed to get him out of her apartment and, most importantly, out of her personal space, had appeared.

The door had almost hit him in the ass on the way out.

You just want her because she's safe. She lives a thousand miles away and she doesn't want a relationship. It's safe to think you want more than sex with her because you barely know her.

That was all true.

Somehow, it wasn't making him wonder *less* about the men in her life since July.

He hadn't *meant* to be celibate. He hadn't met her and thought *she's the one for me forever.* But all the women he'd met since then had just been, well, *less.*

Which was crazy because he barely knew Paige.

"Mitch!"

Linda's voice calling to him from the porch of the big, two-story house, pulled his attention away from his infatuation with the blond who had practically dressed him in this coat and shoved him out the door.

"Hi, Linda." Mitch gave her a smile and climbed the steps.

"Thank you so much for coming over." The older woman gave him a bright, sincere smile.

"Of course. You don't need to go without heat if I can do something about it."

She looked genuinely touched by that. "But you don't even know us."

"Well, I don't need to know you to know you get cold when it's twenty-two degrees outside," he said with a smile.

Twenty-two fucking degrees. He'd never been in weather this cold. It was great. He certainly wouldn't want to work outside in it on a regular basis, but the air was brisk and fresh and he found it exhilarating.

And he didn't have to know Larry and Mike to know that they wouldn't use that word to describe the weather when they were up on those rooftops trying to mend the holes.

He might not feel exhilarated after he climbed up to help them out either.

"I guess you're right," Linda said. "I really didn't want to ask you, but when I heard you were looking at Paige's furnace..."

"It's completely fine," he assured her, feeling a twinge of guilt over Paige's furnace story. It hadn't even been *his* story. Thank God he did know about heating and air-conditioning. And all of the other things the ladies, and town, needed help with.

He shook his head with a grin as he followed Linda into her house. This was exactly how Autre, Louisiana worked. If someone needed something and you could do it or provide it or help with it, you did. Period. No questions. He liked that Appleby and Autre had that in common. Just with a seventy-something-degree temperature difference separating them this time of year.

It also fit that a Landry would be in town for about two hours and would already be involved in the town festival and pitching in to help. His grandparents would be so proud. His dad too. Sean Landry had always told him, "Don't be any trouble. Help out and do your part. Make 'em glad you're there."

Mitch had been doing that since he'd been a little boy.

Linda led Mitch through the house to the kitchen at the back. The entire house was decorated with an apple theme. The sofa had throw pillows with apples stitched on them and a red-and-white blanket draped over the back. The rocking chair near the window had an apple-patterned cushion. The mantel over the fireplace was decorated with a variety of ceramic apples. The entire room looked like a picture postcard.

The rest of the house was similarly decorated. The dining room table had a red runner down the center with a bowl full apples as a centerpiece. The kitchen even had a set of fat-apple canisters on the counter and a large red apple rug covering the wooden floor.

Mitch took it all in as he followed Linda to the basement door and down the steps. The house was a wonderful, old, two story that was well kept, and it was a damned shame this family hadn't been able to be here enjoying it all because their furnace had conked out. He was happy to be here to help.

He wasn't, actually, the Landry most people called for help with things. Leo, his grandfather, or Sawyer, his oldest cousin, were most often the go-tos. There were plenty of others who were always around and willing to help out, of course, and if Leo or Sawyer couldn't be found, Josh, Owen, Ellie, Cora, Maddie, Kennedy… just about any of the others could be. Mitch was the one the Landrys then called. He was in the background. The supporter. The one who had their backs. Quietly. He could always be counted on and his family knew that. He just wasn't in the town's spotlight. Or anyone's spotlight.

Being a Landry, it was pretty easy to play the wallflower, actually. The Landry clan was loud and boisterous and loved to one-up one another. They laughed and teased and loved and joked loud and often, and it was easy to just sit back and be there without adding to the noise.

"Right in here." Linda led him into the room that held the furnace, water heater, and what looked like box upon box of Christmas decorations.

"Great." He moved to the furnace and set the tools down.

"Do you need anything?" Linda asked.

Mitch could tell she was feeling a little guilty about him being here. There was no way he would have been able to let anyone go cold if there was anything he could do about it, but she didn't know him and didn't know that about him. Paige had already turned down Linda's dinner invitation, which was fine; he'd much rather spend his non-furnace-fixing time with Paige, but he also knew the dinner invite had been about repaying him somehow.

He guessed Linda would try to give him money at some point. Which he would, of course, turn down. But she needed to feel she wasn't putting him out entirely.

"I could use somebody to hold the light, actually," he said, pulling out the big work light that Max had included with the tools. That wasn't completely true. He could have found a way to set it up on boxes or something, but having Linda hold it and move it for him would be helpful.

Her face brightened. "Oh, of course." She took the light from him and plugged it into an outlet a few feet away.

"And you can entertain me while I work," he told her with a grin as he shrugged out of the coat and tossed it over a box labeled *front yard blow ups.*

He hadn't noticed blow-up decorations in the front yard so clearly they'd been deflated. Which was too bad. He wanted to get this furnace going again so this family could get back to this house and blow those things up.

"Like singing or something?" she asked with a smile.

"That would work. Do you know any Taylor Swift?"

"You like Taylor Swift?" Linda asked, her smile growing.

"Well, and now you know one of my deepest secrets," he said. "So I'm going to have to do a really good job on this furnace so you don't spread that around."

She laughed. "I do know Taylor Swift, by the way. My oldest daughter is a fan. But you do *not* want me to sing."

"Okay, then something else," he said. "How about town stories."

"Stories about Appleby?" Linda asked. "Oh, I can do that for days."

He chuckled. "I figured." He met her gaze. "I'm from a small town too. I know how that goes."

"And you're interested in our little town?"

He lifted a shoulder. "Seems like a good place." He was supposedly engaged to another woman so he couldn't seem too interested in a certain citizen of this town, but he could hope that Linda knew Paige or at least *about* Paige. For some reason, he had the feeling that Paige didn't let a lot of people close. Of course, she'd spent her life here so people surely knew things *about* her.

"It's a very good place," Linda said with an affectionate smile.

People in Autre definitely got a similar look on their faces when asked about their little town.

He crouched next to the furnace and started pulling tools out of Max's toolbox. "So why a festival in January instead of a holiday festival at Christmastime? Or in the fall when it's warmer?" he asked with a grin, opening the access door on the furnace.

Linda moved in, shining the light over his shoulder on what he was doing.

"Oh, in the fall we have football," she said with a grin. "And Halloween and Thanksgiving and Christmas. People are happy and full of excitement for all of that. But January," she said, shaking her head, "is a long, cold, dark month here in Iowa. We need something to look forward to."

Mitch located the problem in the furnace easily enough and set to work fixing it. "What all happens at the festival?"

"Oh goodness," Linda said.

He could hear the smile in her voice even from behind him.

"It's all about our apples. We have booths with lots of treats. Pies and cobblers and crisps and cookies and cider."

Mitch chuckled. "I'm not sure I've ever fully appreciated all you can do with apples."

"You should certainly stick around. We'll make you love apples. We also have ice skating and sledding and a snowman-building contest and karaoke and sleigh rides and even a snowball fight."

"An organized snowball fight?" Mitch asked. "That sounds interesting. Nobody worried about kids getting hurt, huh?"

She laughed. "It's adults doing the fighting."

He glanced over his shoulder. "No way."

She nodded. "Yep. It gets wild. It happens in the town square. It's kind of like paintball. Each team has a different color snowball —watercolor paints work great—and they have to wear white sweatpants and sweatshirts so you can see the colors show up. That's how you know who wins."

Mitch knew his eyes were wide. "That sounds awesome."

Linda nodded. "It's a lot of fun. There are rules and referees, of course."

He was nodding, thinking about his cousins and friends. They would have a blast with a colored-snowball fight. Or any snowball fight. It was really too bad a snowball would last about a minute in Louisiana.

Maybe he'd just have to haul them all along next year to Iowa...

He quickly shut that down and turned his attention back to Linda's furnace. Paige hadn't even wanted to hear how he hadn't been with another woman in six months. She definitely wouldn't want to hear about him planning to come back next winter. And bringing a bunch of his relatives with him. She clearly was up to her neck in relatives as it was.

"I'm so glad you were able to stop by and help Paige," Linda commented after he'd worked for a few minutes.

He didn't miss how his heart gave an extra *thunk* when Linda said Paige's name. Damn, that wasn't good. "Happy to," he said, trying to sound casual about the first woman he'd felt very *un-casual* about in a very long time. "She's a friend of Tori's. That makes her a friend of mine."

That was true enough. He was very fond of his cousin's fiancée. Everyone who knew Tori was fond of her. She was sweet and funny and had a huge heart and the way she loved Josh made her automatically a Landry family favorite. She'd made Josh happier than Mitch had ever seen him. And Josh was generally a pretty happy guy, actually, so that was saying something.

"Well, Paige is... a little difficult but she's wonderful," Linda said.

Mitch glanced at her before he could stop himself. "Difficult?"

Linda nodded. "I teach with her sister, Amanda, and Paige worries her."

"Her sister?"

"She has two older sisters. Amanda is the oldest."

The one with the kids, likely. So Linda was on Paige's family's side. Wanting Paige to settle down and have a family and be happy. "Paige seems to be doing okay."

She was young. He was aware they were five years apart in age and that at her age the idea of settling down and getting married had been completely laughable to him. It still was, really. His life was good. He had everything he needed. He was happy. Was he a little addicted to a woman who lived too far away to scratch his itch as often as he'd like? Well, yeah, apparently. But if that was the worst thing that ever happened to him, he'd be just fine.

"Oh yes, of course, she's doing okay. Her sister just worries about Paige's decisions."

"What decisions?" he asked. Was it okay to be talking about his fiancée's friend? Well, Linda had brought it up.

"She runs a yoga studio. It's not really an... essential business, you know? And she has cats. Lots of cats. Especially for such a young woman... that's different. Every time someone asks her when she's going to settle down or if she wants to have kids, she gets another one," Linda said. "And she's a vegetarian."

Mitch hid his smile by ducking his head to study the furnace. She got another cat anytime someone asked her about settling down. That was funny.

"I thought the cat thing was an adoption center," he commented, his face in the furnace. Tori had actually filled him in on that when she'd explained how she knew Paige. Tori had been the vet to all of Paige's foster cats.

"It's that," Linda said. "Kind of."

"Kind of?"

"Well, she calls it that, but the process to adopt a cat is crazy," Linda said. "There's a ton of paperwork and she does a home visit and then does follow-up visits after the cat's been adopted for the first six months. Very few people make it past her process."

"Has she ever taken a cat back after letting someone adopt one?"

"She has, actually. Twice."

He couldn't fight his grin this time. That was awesome. "So she's protective of the cats."

"Oh, I think she always intends to keep most of them. That's just her way of pretending to her family that she's *not* a crazy cat lady."

Linda seemed like a nice enough lady. She really did. And he liked her decorating. But he was liking her attitude about Paige less and less all the time.

"Is it a bad thing that she likes cats?" he asked, turning the screw he was tightening a little harder than necessary.

"I suppose not. Her family just worries about some of the things she likes."

"Why?"

"They just worry," Linda said again. "Her business isn't very stable, and she clearly wants to nurture something, but she's choosing cats instead of having a family and she's a vegetarian."

Yeah, she'd mentioned that before too. "So her family worries because they think she's financially vulnerable and that she actually wants children but is filling that need with cats and they're worried she'll..." He shook his head. "I'm not sure why they're worried about the vegetarian thing."

He wasn't sure why they were worried about any of it, frankly.

"Nutrition, of course," Linda said. "They worry about her health."

Right. Well, he knew people who wouldn't understand someone choosing not to eat meat too, but Paige was twenty-two. And clearly in good health. Smart, sassy, confident. She didn't really need people telling her what to do and questioning her decisions.

And suddenly it made sense why she'd gotten annoyed when he'd pointed out that she might have needed to learn a lesson about interacting with her family.

She clearly had a lot of people questioning how she lived her life. She didn't need a guy—especially one she barely knew—telling her that he thought she needed to give her family a break.

He pushed back from the furnace. "All done."

Linda gave a little gasp. "Really? That's it?"

"Yep. Good to go." Mitch stretched to his feet.

"Oh my goodness!" Linda threw her arms around him, nearly knocking him back into the furnace. "Mitch! Thank you so much!"

He patted her back. "Happy to do it."

She pulled back and smiled up at him. "You're a great guy. Tori's really lucky to have you."

For a second he really regretted the lie. It didn't matter in the overall scheme of things, of course. None of these people needed to know what his relationship was to Paige. Or to Tori, for that matter. But he kind of wanted them to.

Except that he and Paige didn't really have a relationship.

But he kind of wanted them to.

At least enough that it would make sense for him to tell all of Appleby to mind their own damned business and let Paige do what she wanted however she wanted to do it.

Of course, one of those things she wanted to do was to let everyone think he was Tori's fiancé so that they didn't hound her about what was going on between *them*. So he would keep playing along.

He smiled at Linda. "Thanks.'"

Linda led him out, chatting more about the festival and how he should invite Tori and how he should be sure to stop by the booth where she and her best friends would be selling caramel apples. He, apparently, gave the correct responses because she smiled and kept talking. But the whole time he was wondering what the chances were of him talking Paige into going to the festival with him and if he'd be able to keep from holding her hand or hugging her or stealing a kiss if they did go together. That would be inappropriate for a guy engaged to her friend.

The alternative was, of course, to just stay at her apartment. In bed.

But for some reason, as amazing as that would be, he suddenly wanted to go to the festival with her. Too. He definitely wanted the bed time. But he was going to be here for a couple of days. And yeah, he wanted to make her pancakes. And he wanted to walk through a winter wonderland festival and drink hot cider with her too.

Maybe showing up early had been a bad idea.

Or maybe it had been the best idea he'd had in a long time.

He drove Paige's car back to her studio and apartment. The streets were clear and dry, but he wondered what it would be like to drive on ice and snow. Might be kind of fun. Could be like driving through a downpour or thick mud, both of which he'd done plenty of.

He had thought about dropping by the houses where Mike

and Larry were working and then swinging by the town square to see if he could figure out what was going on with the electrical wiring down there, but he had to see Paige first.

He'd do all of that. He was used to pulling long days. He simply put together a to-do list at the start of the day and then worked until it was done. He'd do the same here.

But first he needed to see Paige.

He let himself in the side door of the building with the key she'd given him and took the steps up to the second floor two at a time.

He knocked.

It only took a couple of minutes for her to open the door.

She was still wearing the sweatshirt that drove him crazy and those silky pants. She gave him a smile that hit him right in the gut.

He stepped in, nearly on her toes, backing her up, and swinging the door shut behind him.

"How did it—"

He cupped her face and kissed her.

She was clearly startled but only for about two seconds. Then she was gripping his biceps and going on tiptoe and arching close.

This at least made sense.

She was a gorgeous blond with delicious curves who smelled heavenly. *Of course* he wanted her. That was absolutely rational. As were her responses to him. He wasn't too full of himself, not like his cousin Owen, but he knew women found him attractive. He hadn't slept alone for the past six months because there weren't any women interested.

Their attraction was completely reasonable. The rest of it... the wanting to defend her and know her better and *date* her was all completely... unreasonable.

So they'd just focus on the part that he could explain.

He swept his tongue into her mouth as he backed her up against the nearest wall. He slid his hands down to her ass and dipped his knees to fit his cock against her softness.

She gave a quiet moan, and Mitch felt the resultant lick of fire in his belly. He pressed into her, suddenly hungry and completely focused on eliciting that same moan from her again and again.

"Mitch," she whispered raggedly against his mouth as he curled his fingers into her ass.

"Need you, Paige."

"Yes."

That's all he needed to hear. He slid his hand up under the sweatshirt that teased him with glimpses of her skin whenever she moved. He drew it up, making sure his big palm met as much of her silky skin along the way as possible. The soft cotton bunched as he dragged his hand up her rib cage, causing her to suck in a breath, and then around to her back and up to her shoulder blades.

He lifted his head, needing to see everything now. "Arms up," he commanded softly.

She met his eyes as she followed his direction. Her arms stretched up so he could whisk the sweatshirt over her head. He tossed it to the side, his gaze on the gorgeous breasts behind the pale blue sports bra.

He cupped her breasts firmly, the wide band circling her ribs, and crisscrossed over her upper back, and, honestly, he had no idea how to get it off. There were no hooks or snaps or zippers. It occurred to him that he'd never removed a woman's sports bra. He'd seen them, but now that he thought about it, those must have been in photos or something. Most of the bras he'd been up close and personal with were of the tiny, silky, lacy type. That was interesting. Kind of.

Paige must have read that he was stumped in his expression because she laughed lightly and then gripped the bottom of the spandex piece and pulled it up and over her head.

Just pull it off. Noted.

Then he was all about the naked breasts. Because he was really, like most guys, always all about the naked breasts. But Paige happened to have a pair of the best he'd ever seen.

"God, you're gorgeous," he told her gruffly as he studied her.

"Thank you." She reached for one of his hands and brought it to her breast. "Touch me, Mitch."

"Fucking gladly." He cupped her, running his thumb over her hard nipple and relishing her moan.

She leaned into him, kissing him as he played with her nipple, rolling it and plucking and squeezing just hard enough to get a quick gasp and then a louder moan.

He'd just bent his knees and taken a taste when there was a knock at her door.

Five

They both froze.

Then Paige's head fell back against the wall.

"I told you," she said.

Her family. Stopping by as predicted.

He pulled in a breath. Well, fuck.

He straightened. "Okay."

She stepped around him and bent to grab her sweatshirt, pulling it on sans bra. He quickly grabbed that up too. Then she was pushing him toward the bathroom. "Hide in the shower."

"What if they come look in there?"

"Josie was here while you were gone. She brought some leftovers from their dinner last night." Paige rolled her eyes. "She checked out the kitchen. You know, to see if there were two wineglasses or signs that another person was here eating with me. So *this* is Amanda and she'll fake that she needs to borrow clothes so she can check out my bedroom and see if the bed is unmade or if there are men's socks on the floor or something."

He grinned as he stepped into her tiny bathroom. "They're predictable."

"Painfully so," she said with a nod. Then shut the door on him.

He looked around, then down at the bra in his hand, then sighed. And took a seat on the edge of the tub.

"Hi, Amanda." He heard Paige greet her sister.

The apartment was tiny, and he appreciated how well that allowed eavesdropping.

"Hi! I can't stay long but wondering if I could borrow your pink sweater?"

"Oh, a sweater? Sure," Paige said.

Mitch smirked. A sister here to borrow clothes. She'd nailed it.

"Let me go grab it," Paige said.

"I can get it. No problem."

Mitch heard her move past the bathroom door on the way to Paige's bedroom.

"Sure, help yourself to anything," Paige said.

Mitch could almost picture the eye roll.

"What do you need the sweater for?" Paige asked, her voice a bit louder as if she was standing outside the bathroom and calling down the hall.

"I was going to wear it to help at Emily's Girl Scout booth at the festival."

"Oh, okay. So, like under your coat where no one would see it anyway."

Mitch didn't think Paige was buying it. He grinned.

"Well, it will be nice and warm," Amanda answered, her voice louder. Clearly she'd moved closer to the bathroom door again.

"Sure. That makes total sense," Paige said.

Mitch guessed her older sister noted the touch of sarcasm in her voice.

"So... things seem nice and warm up here," Amanda said.

"Yep."

It now sounded like they were standing right outside of the bathroom.

"I mean, you're hardly wearing any clothes."

"I'm wearing what I wear to teach yoga. Which I was just doing."

"So no problem with the heat?"

"Nope, toasty warm, thanks."

"Well, I wouldn't want you to be cold up here. All by yourself."

"I appreciate that. But I've got ways to stay warm."

"Right."

There was a pause. "Okay, so, you have the sweater."

"Yep."

No one was moving. They were definitely still standing outside the bathroom door.

"So I'll see you at the festival maybe."

"And you can't stop over tonight and help the kids?"

"Sorry. I've got stuff to do."

"You don't look like you're getting ready to go out."

"I didn't say I was going out."

Finally, Amanda sighed. "Okay. Thanks for the sweater."

"No problem."

Wow. Mitch had to admit, Paige was good at holding her ground.

He listened to them move to the apartment door and say goodbye. He heard the door shut but waited for Paige to come give him the all clear.

"You can come out," she finally called.

He pulled the door open. She was leaning against the back of the sofa facing him.

"When I came back over here, I meant to tell you that I'm sorry I tried to tell you how to handle your family earlier," he said from the doorway. He needed to tell her this before he got closer to her. Because then he'd touch her. And once he touched her, he'd kiss her. And once he kissed her, he'd be done talking except for telling her to take her clothes off and bend over.

And he really did want to tell her this.

He also really wanted to ask her on a date to the festival, but he *was* going to resist that urge, dammit. Neither of them wanted to date. Even if there wasn't a thousand miles between them making *dating* pretty much impossible.

They wanted to have a hot I'm-only-in-town-for-a-couple-of-days hookup. *Maybe* they would call it friends with benefits, if he could come up with other reasons to come to Iowa from time to time. But other than accompanying Tori on her trips home to see her family, he couldn't really think of anything. And he wasn't sure that tagging along with Josh and Tori for the next twenty years or so made a lot of sense.

Paige crossed her arms and watched him. "What do you mean?"

"Earlier I told you that you needed to maybe give your family a break because they care about you. That was not my place. I don't know your family. I don't know how things work with your family. I don't get to tell you how to act or react with them. I'm sorry about that."

Her eyebrows were up by the time he finished.

She dropped her arms. "Wow."

He stepped out of the bathroom. "I was going to go over and check in at the town square but I had to come over and tell you that first. And then..."

"You kissed me." She gave him a little smile.

He nodded. "Well, that was your fault."

"My fault? You started it."

"No. You opened the door."

"I let you in."

He took a step closer. "Yeah, but that meant you were within reach. And whenever you're within reach, I kind of forget about everything else but touching you."

She took a little breath, her smile fading. But she was still watching him intently. "Now, see, usually when guys say stuff like that, I find it pretty intense and consider it a red flag and immediately want to get some space."

He tucked his hands into his pockets and nodded.

"But with you… I don't want space."

Mitch felt his chest tighten. "You pushed me out of this apartment pretty quick when you found out I hadn't been with any other women."

She pressed her lips together and nodded.

"You didn't think that was pretty intense?"

She nodded again.

"And it made you want space, right?"

She took a breath. "I pushed you out before I could tell you that I haven't been with anyone since we were together either." She paused. "*That* made me want space."

Mitch let that sink in.

She hadn't been with anyone else either.

She hadn't been with anyone else either.

She hadn't fucking been with anyone else either.

He felt a little like beating his chest and shouting, *Yes!*

But he simply cleared his throat and said, "I'm not going to say I'm sorry."

One corner of her mouth curled up. "What would you be sorry for?"

"Ruining you for all other men."

The other corner of her mouth tipped up and she shook her head. "That's not what I said."

He nodded. "But that's what happened."

"I wouldn't put it quite that way."

"I would."

She lifted a brow. "Well, you would be wrong."

"I don't think so."

"So I ruined *you* for all other women?" she asked, crossing her arms again.

"Yeah. I'm pretty sure."

Her eyes widened. "Now *that* makes me want space."

He shook his head and stepped toward her. "You can't ruin me and then push me away."

"Oh, I think I can."

"That's just cruel."

He stopped right in front of her. He didn't touch her. But he saw her take a quick breath in. Her arms were still crossed, but she was watching him with wide eyes, her pupils dilated.

"This can't get serious," she said quietly.

"I know."

"We live too far apart."

"I know."

"And I'm... too young to be serious."

"I know."

"And I'm a vegetarian who doesn't have a real job and collects cats."

Yeah, all of those life choices that made her happy that everyone had been judging and questioning and being *concerned* about. "I know."

"I just want to do my own thing. How I want to. When I want to. I don't like explaining everything I do, and I don't like defending my choices that don't really have anything to do with anyone else and don't hurt anyone."

Mitch felt his chest tighten again. A woman had never done that to him. Well, a woman he wanted to sleep with anyway. The women he loved—his cousins and aunts and grandmother—made him feel protective and like he wanted to fix things. But he'd never felt that way over a woman he was dating. Certainly not a woman he'd had a one-night stand with. Which was what Paige Asher was essentially.

"I know," he said again. "You shouldn't have to explain yourself or defend your choices."

"So a long-distance relationship would be difficult," she said. "You'd wonder what I was doing when we weren't together. You might not like it if I went out with another guy. And I wouldn't want to explain any of that either."

No, he really fucking wouldn't like it if she went out with another guy. And no, it really wouldn't be his damned business.

He nodded. "You're right about that too."

"Which part?" she asked.

"All of it."

"You wouldn't like it?"

"Absolutely not."

Her expression was *I knew it*. "But I shouldn't have to explain that. We would be seeing each other, what? Twice a year? Maybe?"

He nodded. "You shouldn't have to explain that."

"So it would be better to just not think this was anything more than a hookup while you're in town with Tori." She actually sounded a little sad about that.

Which made sense to him. He definitely felt a little sad about it. Which was really dumb. What had he thought this could possibly be?

"We should really get on with this hookup thing, then," he said, reaching for her and catching the front of her sweatshirt in his fingers and pulling her up from the back of the couch.

She went willingly, and he whipped her shirt over her head before bringing her in to kiss her. She slipped her hands under the edge of his t-shirt, running her hands up his sides and making his skin heat instantly. She traced her fingertips over the ridges of his abs, sliding up to his chest and then his shoulders, gripping them and using them for leverage to arch closer.

Mitch let her go long enough to jerk his shirt over his head, then lifted her against him, feeling her breasts pressing into his chest.

Her arms went around his neck, molding her to his body as he gripped her ass and walked them to the breakfast bar that separated the living room from the kitchen. He set her on the edge of the counter and pulled his mouth away to kiss down to the breast he'd left wet and needy when her sister had knocked.

He sucked and licked, making her wiggle against him. Her fingers dug into his shoulders. Her pants and gasps heightening his own need.

He tucked his fingers into the top of her yoga pants and started to slide them down.

"Lift up, sweetheart."

She did, immediately—he really did love how compliant she was to his commands during sex—and he slid the pants down her legs.

She didn't wear panties with her yoga pants.

He paused, studying her completely nude body.

"Panties ride up and pinch," she said as explanation.

"I'm a huge fan of yoga, if I haven't mentioned that before," he said.

She smirked. Then spread her legs farther. "Because of yoga, I have fantastic core control. Which includes my pelvic floor," she informed him.

"That might be the hottest thing anyone's ever said to me," he told her, stepping between her knees.

She laughed. "That's maybe a little sad."

He cupped her ass—he really loved her ass—and dragged his beard against her jaw. "Well, maybe I should explain that what I *heard* you say was *Mitch, I can grip your cock and milk it with my pussy to the point it will make your eyes cross, and you might not be able to walk afterward.*"

He felt her throat work as she swallowed hard. "Well, when you put it *that way...*"

He chuckled, kissing her neck, then biting down gently on the spot where it curved into her shoulder. "I mean, you *can* grip me like a fist with that sweet pussy, right, Paige?"

"Oh... yeah," she said, breathlessly.

"Show me." He moved his hand down along her thigh, then shifted his hips so he could move his hand to cup her, sliding his middle finger over her clit.

She moaned and tipped her head back, moving her thighs even wider.

She was so sexy. So open. Not just literally opening her legs, but in this, at least, she was willing to be vulnerable. She wasn't trying to cover any part of her body or hide anything. She was bare naked on her kitchen counter with daylight spilling in through the big window across the room.

Of course, she had nothing to worry about. She was gorgeous. Tight and trim, with lots of smooth, sweet skin and curves in all the right places.

He circled her clit, loving the way she tried to get even closer to his touch. She braced one hand on the counter behind her, using it to lift and press closer. He lifted his head to watch her face as he teased her. She was so responsive. Hungry and greedy and yet had been so willing to please him in every way last time they'd been together as well.

Watching her, he moved his hand so his thumb continued to rub that sweet spot as his thick middle finger slid into her.

His knees nearly buckled. As if *she* were touching *him*. Her pussy was tight and so fucking hot. Wet. Sweet. She did, indeed, grip his finger as he pressed inside.

Her throaty *yes* made his cock ache and he pumped his finger deeper.

"Oh God, Mitch."

He added a second finger. "Show me that amazing core, girl," he told her.

Her head was back and her eyes closed, but she smiled at that. Then tightened her inner muscles around his finger.

Damn. His cock was screaming *mine*. He wanted to plunge deep and hard. Then he wanted to fuck her slow and steady. He wanted to feel all of that sweet heat gripping and clenching around him.

Just then there was a knock at the door.

They both stiffened in shock.

No. *No.* Not now. They couldn't just leave her the hell alone?

Her thighs instinctively started to close. Not that they could with him standing between them.

He put his mouth to her ear. "You're not going anywhere."

His finger was still buried inside her. He moved it in and out to remind her.

"But…"

"Shh…" he coached softly. "I can't let you go, sweetheart. I can't leave this sweet body like this. I need to feel you come apart."

Her pussy tightened around his finger. Yeah, she wanted this too.

There was another knock.

Her body stiffened but he stroked her—her back… and her pussy. "Ignore them. Concentrate on me."

Wow. That sounded pretty damned great. Certainly at this moment, but just in general. Maybe she just needed someone who could make her not think about them and their seemingly constant demands and "worry" that she was doing things wrong.

He kept his mouth against her ear. "I love your body. I could lose myself in you for days." He moved his fingers as he talked, feeling her body relax and soften around his fingers and against him.

He thought he heard another knock, then he heard, "Paige!"

"I want to make you come like this," he said in her ear, circling her clit. He bent to take a nipple in is mouth, sucking hard as he pumped his fingers in and out. Then he said, "Then I want to turn you around, bend you over this counter, and fuck you from behind."

"Yes, I want that," she said, her pussy tightening.

Okay, good, she was with him.

He put his mouth on hers. "But you have to stay quiet," he told her. "Can you come quietly?" he asked, kissing her before letting her answer.

"I don't know," she said, teasing back, even though her voice was ragged.

"Let's try it. I don't mind if the world hears me make you come apart," he confessed.

"You can't let up on me a little? So I don't scream?"

He loved that she was teasing him even as she was on the brink of an orgasm.

"I can't let up on you," he said, shaking his head and looking into her eyes. "I need you dreaming about me when I'm not here."

She wet her lips. "I don't think you have to worry."

He liked that. Too much. He gave her a wicked grin. "Prepare yourself for some *very* dirty Zoom calls."

Her cheeks actually got pink. She was bare-assed-naked on the kitchen counter with his hand in the most intimate place it could be, but she was blushing about the idea of a dirty Zoom call? He grinned.

"That's not really having space," she pointed out.

"Nope," he agreed. He wanted zero space.

He'd worry about that later.

Then he circled her clit and she let out a lusty sigh. "Okay."

"Okay to the Zoom call? Or the quiet orgasm now?" He thrust his fingers deep.

"Both." Her eyes were shut again.

"Deal." Then he bent his knees, pulled her ass to the edge of the counter, and put his mouth on her clit, licking and sucking as he finger fucked her.

"Oh, oh, oh…"

He looked up. She was gripping the edge of the counter, her eyes shut, her bottom lip between her teeth.

"Be quiet, sweetheart," he coached with a grin.

He had no idea if whoever had stopped by was still outside her door. And he didn't care.

He sucked on her clit again and curled his fingers and pumped in and out and suddenly her hand flew to his head, gripping his hair as her thighs tightened around him and her pussy clenched and she let out a long, but very soft, "Yessssss."

He released her clit with a gentle lick and then slowly eased his fingers from her body. He looked up at the most beautiful sight.

She was leaning back, propped on her extended arm, her chest rising and falling with her rapid breaths. Her eyes were shut, her cheeks flushed, and she had a smile on her face.

He rose and her eyes opened. She watched as he lifted his fingers to his mouth and licked the taste of her from them.

"Wow, that's dirty," she said appreciatively.

He just grinned. "You're amazing."

"I'm—"

Her phone started ringing.

She stopped. Rolled her eyes. Sighed. And then laughed. "In trouble."

"That's whoever was at the door?" he asked. Jesus, these people were relentless.

She nodded. "Or my mother wondering why that person told her I wasn't here."

She pushed him back and hopped to the floor, again grabbing her sweatshirt and pulling it on. It didn't cover much. Definitely not the sweet ass he was obsessed with.

Her phone stopped ringing.

"So the bending you over the counter..." he said.

She tossed him a mischievous look over her shoulder. "Well, you did talk about the whole delayed-satisfaction thing." Her gaze dropped to his fly. "But I guess that's more *you* than *me* at the moment."

He nodded, lowering his voice. "Maybe I should barricade the door, hide your phone, and put you on your knees."

Her breath hitched and her eyes heated. "Maybe..."

Her phone started ringing again. With a sigh she reached for it. "Hello?"

She paused, listening.

"No, I'm fine, why?"

Pause.

"I couldn't come to the door."

Pause. She looked at the ceiling.

"Because I couldn't. I don't just sit around here waiting for one of you to stop by, you know."

She frowned as she listened to the reply.

"Of course I know that."

She listened again, taking a deep breath. "Yes, I have plenty of eggs. Have him come back over."

She disconnected and gripped her phone tightly, before meeting Mitch's gaze. "You want to hide in my bedroom closet this time? Since Amanda was already in there, my Uncle Tim won't check in there when he stops by to install my new showerhead."

"You need a new shower head?" Mitch asked. "I could install—"

"No," she stopped him. "I don't need a new showerhead. But that's a good reason to check the bathroom for signs of a 'guest'. My sisters already checked the other rooms." She looked around. "I mean, everyone can see the living room."

Wow, these people would impress his family if he were being honest. All of this was Landry-level meddling.

"Well, how about I head to the town's square now?" he asked, pulling his shirt on. "That way I'm *really* not here and I have an alibi."

She smiled but sighed. "I really prefer you here without the shirt on."

"Ditto."

"But, yeah, okay."

"The square is close enough to walk to," he said. "I'll slip up the alley and won't even need to move your car."

She frowned. "It's really cold, Mitch. And you'll need the toolbox, right?"

He arched a brow. "I can carry a toolbox four blocks."

"But... it's cold. You've got Louisiana blood. You might not make it a block before you're an ice cube."

"Sweetheart—" He pulled her up against him and kissed her. "That Louisiana blood means I've got enough stubborn and cayenne in my system to keep me going for a long time in the cold."

She went on tiptoe to kiss him again, then said, "Well, maybe get *a little* cold so I can warm you up when you get back."

"I'll *never* be too warm to not need you warming me up." He squeezed her ass, then let her go, grabbing the coat he was borrowing and heading for the door. "If I swing by to see how Mike and Larry are doing too, would that give your family time to send everyone over that needs to stop by and check on you?"

She narrowed her eyes and put her hands on her hips. "It's bugging you that there's work that needs to be done and you're not helping, isn't it?"

"Well, I mean, it's *cold* out, and those boys probably haven't eaten enough gumbo in their day to counteract it."

She laughed. "Fair enough." Then she nodded. "Yeah, I think Tim will stop by and then maybe my grandpa. He'll want to check the furnace and be sure you did a good job."

Mitch paused with a hand on her doorknob. "Your grandpa can fix furnaces? Will he think it's weird you didn't just ask him in the first place?"

She shook her head. "He'll just roll his eyes and tell me that I don't have to be so damned independent all the time and that I can ask family to help out and I don't always have to hire help."

"You hire help instead of asking your family?" He immediately regretted the question and his raised eyebrows.

She frowned. "I do. It's my business and my apartment. I can handle taking care of it."

"You're an independent little thing, aren't you?"

She lifted her chin. "I am."

"Noted."

He was *not* used to that. Everyone he knew leaned on everyone else he knew. That was just the way of it. But *everyone* helped *everyone* out. Each person did their part. If someone couldn't fix a furnace, they could sure as hell make an amazing étouffée, or would help with plumbing or painting, or would do your laundry. Or they might just tell you when you needed to pull your head out of your ass when you needed it. Which was, honestly, a lot more helpful than being able to fix a furnace. Anyway, it wasn't as if anyone was a freeloader or getting away with anything.

"And don't call me a little thing," Paige added. "That sounds patronizing as hell."

Also noted. He nodded. Then gave her a little grin. "You know, with that attitude, you'd fit right in with the bayou girls."

"Oh yeah?"

"They don't take any shit from anyone."

She tipped her head. "And you respect that?"

"Completely." He shrugged. "It's what I know. Of course, if I *hadn't* respected it, my grandma would have smacked me upside the back of my head. *And* made me clean up after the crawfish boils for a month. By myself."

"Big job?"

"Very."

She smiled. "Well, with *that* attitude, I might let you stick around."

He really wanted to. *A lot.*

But as the words hung between them, and he felt that she was thinking about maybe clarifying that she meant *for a couple of days,* he quickly pulled on his coat, gave her a wink, and stepped out the door before she could.

He was in so much trouble.

Six

He thought about that as he walked with Max's toolbox in hand on the way to the town square. He *didn't* want Paige to point out that this was a couple-of-days-only fling? Hell, shouldn't *he* have been the one making sure that point was made and made often? That they were absolutely in agreement there? That's how it would have been with any other woman.

That's the way it *had been* with every other woman.

But this one was... different. That was the best word he could come up with and it wasn't a great word, honestly. He was intrigued by her. Intrigued enough that these few days with her didn't feel like enough.

So what did that mean?

He thought about that as he checked the wiring for the multiple small booths and the large main stage that dotted the grassy area in the center of town. The paved walkways that crisscrossed the space had been cleared of snow, and the pine trees that were scattered through the square were decorated with twinkle lights. Those along with the ones adorning the wooden booths and the front of the stage were all dark at the moment, however.

As was the lighted APPLE FESTIVAL sign that hung from the archway that declared this the Appleby City Park.

Linda had said there would be music and heaters that needed to be plugged in to keep cider and other treats warm. He also noted tall standing heaters placed among the booths for people to gather around in case things got especially chilly during the festival.

Mitch shook his head. He'd fixed a few furnaces in Louisiana but couldn't say there was much call for large outdoor heaters.

"You must be Mitch."

He turned at the male voice behind him. He smiled at the older man approaching. "Yes, I am. You were warned?"

The man laughed and extended his hand as he came to stop. "I'm Phil Custer. I agreed to help set up the booths and stage and everything here. I was the one that ran into the no-power problem."

The man was in his late sixties or so and wore his long gray hair pulled back into a ponytail under his stocking cap. Even though it was early January and the ground was covered with snow, the man's skin was tanned and wrinkled in the familiar way of so many people who worked outdoors.

"I'm happy to take a look," Mitch said, shaking Phil's hand.

"Good deal. I'm good with hauling and building but not so much with electrical and such," the other man said. "I was an over-the-road trucker all my life. I can look at most motors and know what I'm doing and I thought I could maybe figure this wiring problem out, but this is a little beyond me." He looked around the square with a grin.

"Well, no guarantees that I can make it work either. I know motors and wires and plumbing and all of that," Mitch said. "But sometimes shit just breaks and you gotta start over."

Phil nodded. "That's for sure. Really hoping that's not the case here though. Not sure we've got time to rewire all of it."

Mitch looked around. There was a lot to check out. But if *nothing* was working, it had to be a pretty centralized problem.

Phil showed him around and he got to work.

And thinking.

A long-distance relationship? Was that what he wanted with Paige? Could they make that work? Did he even have the first clue how to do that?

No, he didn't have the first clue. But yes, he thought maybe he did want it. Not the distance so much, but Paige. He wanted her.

He wasn't a relationship guy, really. Short distance or long distance. But hell, maybe long distance was the way to go. He wouldn't have to be sweet and thoughtful every day that way.

By the time he'd found the wiring problem, fixed it, and had the square lit up, the sun had dropped behind the horizon. The glow of the white lights reflecting off the snow made him smile.

"Nicely done!" Phil said, joining him in front of the stage.

"Thanks. Looks good."

"It really does, thanks to you. Everyone will be so happy to know that things will be ready and working tomorrow. Thank you." Phil clapped him on the shoulder.

Mitch couldn't help his grin. This felt good. It was just some electrical wiring. It had taken him less than an hour. But this kind of work always made him feel good.

It was productive and it mattered. It was behind-the-scenes stuff. Stuff that most people attending the festival wouldn't even think about, but it made a difference. *Without* it, people would notice. They'd notice the cold cider and the lack of light and music. Fixing that wiring mattered. Just like fixing broken pipes at his grandma's restaurant and repairing tires on the bus that brought tourists to his cousins' swamp boat tours and repairing the motors on the boats all mattered.

It was stuff that the tourists, and sometimes even his family, didn't really think about but without which, things wouldn't work and wouldn't be as good as they could be.

He didn't need recognition for it. Just seeing those lights

glowing and knowing that tomorrow the cider would be hot was enough for him.

"My pleasure," he told Phil.

"If you're going to keep working outside in January, you need to get yourself a good pair of gloves," Phil said, noticing Mitch's red hands.

Mitch rubbed them together and then shook them. "I'll admit I didn't come prepared to be outside in this weather."

"Well, here." Phil pulled his own gloves off. "Damn, boy, I'm sorry I didn't notice before now." He handed the gloves to Mitch.

"Oh, I couldn't have worked with those on anyway," Mitch said, holding up a hand. The bulky gloves would have gotten in the way of the fine work he'd needed to do on the wires.

"They can warm you up now, then."

"I can't take your gloves."

"I've got a dozen pairs at home," Phil said with a laugh, waggling the gloves. "These were just the first I grabbed. I'm not attached."

Mitch grinned.

"And," Phil went on, "I'm guessing you might have more need for them. Once people find out that you saved the festival, you'll have more people with things that need fixing calling you up."

Mitch wasn't so sure about that, but he had planned to stop and see how Larry and Mike were doing on the roofs about two blocks away. He took the gloves. "Okay, if you're sure."

"You bet," Phil said.

Mitch pulled the gloves on, then shook the other man's hand.

"See you at the festival tomorrow," Phil said.

Mitch just nodded. He hoped so. If Paige wanted to keep him in bed all day he wouldn't exactly object, but he was now very interested in this festival. Hell, he even kind of liked the cold weather. He wasn't sure he could live and work here, but if he had a hot, sassy blond at home to warm him up after a day in the cold, it might not be so bad.

He was actually thinking about how he could *live* here?

He was definitely in trouble.

Because as nice as this little town seemed and as charming as the snow was, he couldn't leave his family. They needed him. Sure, they could find someone else to do the things he did for them, but... he wanted to be the one doing it. He owed them everything, and he wanted to take care of them in return.

But Paige might like the heat...

Fuck. He had to stop thinking about either of them relocating. That was ridiculous.

He headed up the block, determined to focus on fixing the roofs and then going back and stripping her naked and stopping all this craziness that included words like *long term* or *committed* or *relationship*.

"Hey, guys," Mitch greeted as two older men came toward him across the snowy front yard of one of the big old houses that Max had described to him.

"You must be Mitch," one of them said with a smile.

"Yeah. Can I lend a hand?"

"Actually, we're done."

The men stopped in front of him, looking pleased.

"Already?" Mitch asked, looking up at the roof of the house behind them.

"Seems some of the ladies mentioned to their husbands and sons about a total stranger offering to help us out and they felt guilty, and a bunch showed up to help us get things done."

Mitch grinned at that. "I didn't make the offer to guilt anyone else into helping."

One of the men laughed. "Even better. You just pricked at their consciences."

"But we appreciate your willingness," the other man said. "Decent of you."

Mitch shrugged. "If I'm able, there's no reason not to."

"Funny that you're not from the Midwest," the taller of the two said. "That's a pretty Midwestern attitude."

Mitch smiled. "Maybe Iowa and Louisiana aren't that different."

Both men nodded. "Maybe not. Nice to know."

They parted ways, also mentioning that they'd see Mitch at the festival the next day.

It seemed everyone in town showed up to the event. Mitch could understand that too. Autre, Louisiana was the same way. If there was a get-together, a party, a celebration... or just a random Friday night... nearly the whole town would turn out.

The crawfish boils at his grandma's bar was one such event. Tourists and locals alike gathered around the ramshackle building and ate fresh-caught crawfish, corn, and potatoes, drank beer and moonshine, and just generally celebrated the important things in life—friends, family, good food, good music, the great outdoors, and the roots and history of the area.

It seemed very much like Appleby. Families stayed close, friends had known each other most of their lives, the community came together in good times and bad, and people appreciated tradition and the little things. Or the things that seemed little but actually mattered a lot.

Paige would be at home in Autre. Sure, there was a huge, noisy, and nosy family to contend with, but he'd love to see her chatting with the other women in his life, charming the men, clutching the side of an airboat and laughing as he opened it up on the bayou, tipping back a mason jar of moonshine, dancing to some good old Cajun music.

Of course, he'd also love the alone time he could imagine clearly. Taking her down to the bank to lie in the bed of his truck to look at the stars. Passing a lazy Sunday afternoon, napping with her in the hammock in his backyard. Cuddling on his couch watching a movie on a Friday night. Going for breakfast at his grandma's before heading out to work. Sneaking in a quickie over his lunch break. Sitting on his front porch with sweet tea and watching the lightning bugs come out.

He was getting incredibly sappy. And too comfortable with how easy it was to picture all of that.

With a sigh, he pulled his phone from his pocket as he hit the sidewalk in front of the yoga studio. He opened Paige's car and tucked the toolbox behind the front seat. Then he slid into the driver's seat so he didn't freeze his nuts off while talking to Chase.

Because, yeah, it was time to call his buddy. The one who was just starting a long-distance relationship himself.

But Chase wouldn't be alone. No one was really ever alone in Autre unless they grabbed a boat when no one was looking, headed out on the bayou, and found a quiet nook.

City boy Chase Dawson, however, would not be able to do that. He was mostly hopeless with boats. Though if he and his stupid frat-boy friends hadn't stolen one of the Boys of the Bayou swamp tour boats and crashed it into the dock, his sister would have never met her true love, Sawyer, and Chase wouldn't have been hanging out in Autre repairing the dock and becoming smitten with the cute, nerdy alligator conservationist Bailey.

The girl he was now head over heels for.

Mitch hit the button that would call Chase, wondering if he was going to regret this. Chase wasn't going to be able to convincingly talk Mitch *out* of trying a long-distance deal with Paige.

Chase was going to medical school at Georgetown while Bailey worked in Louisiana at her dream job. They were going to do the long-distance thing, with as-frequent-as-possible trips between DC and Autre, with the hopes for a residency in New Orleans.

Mitch expected that Chase would eventually be a small-town Southern doctor seeing everything from fish hooks stuck through thumbs to chicken pox to cancer. And he was going to love it. Which was hilarious considering the guy had gotten pretty green the first time he'd seen them cleaning fish or when Leo, Mitch's grandpa, had pulled a rusty nail out of his own foot.

The born-rich city boy was going to have to toughen up some, but Mitch was thrilled to think his friend would eventually be around for good. It was crazy how well they'd bonded. They had almost nothing in common, and Mitch was about four years older than Chase. Still, they'd quickly become friends, and Mitch missed the dumbass when he was back in DC.

"Dude," Chase greeted on the second ring. "I told you that you should never unzip your pants outdoors in Iowa in January. That's dangerous, man. But you just don't listen."

"So no sympathy at all?" Mitch asked with a grin. "No magic cure?"

"We're gonna have to chop it off," Chase said, sounding sad. Fake sad, but still. "Good thing you had so much fun with it when you did."

Mitch shuddered. "My dick is fine. But the fact that it's on your mind so much is really touching. Weird. But touching."

"Never use the word *touching* when talking about me and your dick in the same breath." Chase paused. "Actually, how about we not talk about your dick and me in the same breath at all?"

Mitch laughed. "Well, I just have to say, if I got frostbite on my dick, your phone would be the first one I'd send the photos to."

"Trust me, that would go out to all my med-school friends, and we'd talk about how guys like you will keep guys like me in business."

Mitch suddenly had a pang of homesickness. Which was strange. He hadn't been gone *that* long. And Appleby was a great place. And Paige was here.

But the thoughts of Paige down on the bayou with him and his family and friends had sunk in deep and quick. He wanted to take her down there. To have her meet everyone. To see how she reacted to cruising along the bayou. To see how much she'd love the otters. Yes, otters.

The Boys of the Bayou's main dock had been adopted by a river otter they'd named Gus. Gus had then gotten a girlfriend. And then they'd had a family. And those otters had moved into a more formal home outside of Leo's old trailer, complete with a plastic swimming pool and slides and everything. Of course, they spent time with animal-crazy Tori and Mitch's cousin Kennedy as well.

That was all temporary though. Mitch was in the process of building a bigger, better enclosure for them as a part of a new side business for the Boys of the Bayou.

Yeah, he wanted to see Paige playing with otters. Definitely. Maybe even more than he wanted to see her in short shorts. So that was… idiotic.

He scrubbed a hand over his face. "I do have a problem," he said to Chase.

"Does it involve your dick?"

"N…" Then he thought about that. It was perfectly fine to include talk of Paige and his dick in the same breath. "I mean… kind of."

"The girl," Chase said.

Mitch huffed out a breath. He shouldn't have been surprised Chase figured that out. "Yeah. Paige."

"You *just* got there, man."

"Sounds familiar, right?" Mitch asked. He'd been shocked by how quickly Chase had been distracted and fascinated by Bailey.

Chase sighed. "Yeah."

Mitch could hear the grin in his voice. He'd fallen fast and hard for Bailey. In spite of telling himself—and Mitch—over and over that it made no sense. Chase and Bailey were total opposites. Total. Opposites. And Bailey had been pretty unimpressed with Chase's charm and good looks and money. All things that Chase was used to using to get his way with women. Well, with everyone.

Add into that the fact that Bailey and Chase hadn't even been able to execute their first kiss without almost breaking a nose and some toes, and they seemed like a total mess.

But Mitch could tell that Chase was happier than he'd ever been.

"So you're calling for love advice," Chase said.

Oh shit. Chase had just raised his voice slightly. That meant someone, or more than one someone, was close by. Which meant that someone, or more than one someone, was about to chime in.

"No worries, I'm here!" Mitch heard Owen Landry, one of his cousins, say.

"Where are you and Owen?" Mitch asked, praying they'd snuck down to the dock with a couple of beers to escape the chaos that was every Landry family get-together.

"Ellie's," Chase said.

There was a rise in noise on Chase's end of the phone, and Mitch realized that Chase had ducked into the back room or just outside to take the call initially. And now he was back in the main room of Ellie's bar. Where *everyone* would be.

"You're a bastard," Mitch told him.

"This will just keep me from having to repeat everything later," Chase said with a laugh.

No one had a big enough house for them all to really spread out and chat and eat. They'd gather together for gift opening, practically sitting on top of one another, but for meals and hanging out, they'd all move over to the bar.

The building was really just an extension of Ellie's home in many ways. Most family meals were served there, and every member of the family stopped in at the bar at some point during the day. If Ellie and Cora, her best friend and business partner, didn't see everyone at least once a day, they got worried and sent someone to hunt the missing person down. And drag them in for some grits. Because grits were good for everything—happy, hungry, feeling sick, feeling awesome, lonely, sad, or newly in love.

"So what do you need to know?" Owen asked.

Mitch realized he was now on speakerphone. Great.

"I just..." He blew out a breath. What the hell? Owen was also madly in love. With a sassy, smart, too-good-for-him woman named Maddie. Owen might actually have some advice. "I guess I'm thinkin' about a long-distance relationship."

"They suck, man," Chase said.

"You don't even know," Mitch told him. "You *just* officially got together with Bailey."

"And I already know it's going to suck," Chase told him.

"But you're gonna do it anyway?"

"Well... yeah." Chase sounded like that was a really stupid question.

Maybe it was.

"Why's it gotta be long distance?" Owen asked.

"Because..." Well, fuck. Because it would be crazy for one of them to move to be with the other at this point.

"If you're doin' things right, she's not gonna want to live without you," Owen said. "So start doin' things right."

"If I remember correctly, Maddie was ready to move back to California even after *you* were doing things."

Owen laughed. "'Cause I wasn't doin' things *right*."

"I'm not sure I want details about what you were doing wrong," Mitch said dryly.

"Oh, nothin' like *that*," Owen said, clearly catching his meaning. "Trust me."

"So what?" Mitch asked, hoping he wasn't making a mistake.

"I just had to figure out that living anywhere *with* her was better than living at all *without* her. It just works out."

"So your advice is to move to Iowa to be with a woman I've known for like two days. Other than a few months of texting."

"What's the worst that can happen?" Owen asked. "It doesn't work out and you move back here."

"That's..." He really should have finished that thought with *crazy*. Or *ridiculous* would have fit too. But Owen had a point. Didn't he? Mitch could move to Iowa. He wasn't in medical school. He didn't own a business he couldn't move. He had a huge family that he'd miss like hell, but was this thing with Paige at least worth giving some more time to?

"I'm good," Owen said. "I know."

"She hasn't exactly asked me to stay," Mitch said.

"Well, she can't really *keep* you from moving somewhere.

You're a grown man. She can't keep you out of Appleby," Chase pointed out.

"That doesn't seem a little stalkerish?"

"Why do you boys always make this all so difficult?"

There was now a new voice in the conversation. And Mitch would know that voice anywhere.

Ellie. His grandmother. The tough, no-bullshit matriarch of the Landry family.

"Tell her what you're thinkin', Mitchell," Ellie said. "Don't be weird about it. Just say, *I think I'm crazy about you, and I want to find out if this can work out.* For God's sake."

Mitch could picture her rolling her eyes at them all. He also knew she had her hands planted on her skinny hips.

"You all make this seem like some huge mysterious, magical thing. You don't have to wait for planets to line up or for some big sign like your favorite song to play just as the full moon comes up over the hill when the scent of lilacs drifts through your window."

Now she was most definitely rolling her eyes.

Owen laughed. "You and this family are the biggest fuckin' romantics in the entire universe, Ellie."

Yes, they all called their grandmother Ellie and their grandfather Leo. Because *all* of their grandparents on both sides of the family lived in town, so simply referring to them as "grandma" and "grandpa" had never been specific enough.

"Sure, we're romantic," Ellie said. "We know when it's right and we're willing to go big when that happens."

It was true that the Landrys were known for their grand, romantic gestures. It was countywide legend, actually. But he supposed that didn't mean they thought the falling-in-love part was all that complicated.

"Well, I won't tell Cora that you think her love potion is bullshit," Chase said.

Cora made all kinds of "potions". She also made balms and salves and other homemade "cures". The thing was, even skeptical physician-to-be Chase had to admit the stuff worked. Mitch fully expected Chase to incorporate some of those things into his medical practice when he came back to Autre for good.

"Oh, she knows it's bullshit," Ellie said. "Who would believe a love potion? You can't *make* love happen."

"But... wait... what else of hers is bullshit?" Chase asked.

Mitch snorted and heard Owen laugh as well.

"Oh honey," Ellie said, and Mitch could picture her putting her hand on Chase's cheek.

"The only stuff that's bullshit is the stuff that doesn't work," Ellie told Chase placatingly.

"But..." Chase was clearly thinking on all of the things he'd tried while in Autre. "All of it worked. Didn't it?"

"Then I guess it's all real," Ellie told him.

"That's not how science works," Chase said. He sounded tired.

The Landrys had that effect on people. Chase was still getting used to them all.

Ellie laughed. "Oh well, we aren't talking about science."

"Then what are we talking about?"

"Love."

"Love isn't science?" Chase asked.

"Is it?" Ellie challenged in return. "You tellin' me that what you're feeling for that beautiful accident-waitin'-to-happen over there is all just synapses and endorphins?"

"Well..." was Chase's only response.

Mitch assumed that Bailey, who was indeed a beautiful accident-waiting-to-happen, was across the room and Chase was now gazing at her adoringly.

Mitch shook his head even though he was grinning.

"Exactly," Ellie said after a moment. "You've probably had your hormones get all stirred up before. Chemistry and whatever. But what you feel for Bailey is different. And I don't think you can explain it with science."

"But," Chase tried again, "science is real."

"Well, of course it's real," Ellie said in her no-shit tone of voice. "Germs and stuff are real. You come out of the bathroom without washing your hands or cough on my bar without covering your mouth, and I'll slap you upside the head and cut you off from gumbo for a week."

"So..." But Chase didn't add on to that start.

"So science and things beyond science can both be true at the same time," Ellie said.

"Then Cora's potions and creams do actually work?" Chase asked.

Mitch knew his friend was rubbing his head.

Ellie blew out an exasperated breath. "I'm tellin' you that you boys are bein' nitpicky dumbasses."

"Dumbasses?" Chase repeated. "To want to prove something is true?"

"Good lord," Ellie muttered. "Do you need a research paper to tell you something is working if you can see it and feel it with your own eyes and heart?" she asked.

"If millions of people use condoms and there are fewer women gettin' knocked up, then you know that the condoms are working, right? If people start wearin' seat belts and more people walk away from car crashes, you know the seat belts are working. If you burn your hand and put a salve on it and it feels better the next day, then it worked to make your hand feel better. And if you find a woman who makes you think about turning your whole life upside down to be with her, then you're falling in love with her." Ellie's voice softened. "Nothing changes a life more than love does."

"I..." Chase trailed off. "Yeah. I guess you're right."

Ellie scoffed. "Of course I'm right. I'm old. I know a lot of shit by now."

There was a pause and the sound of shuffling on the other end of the phone.

"Well, there you go," Chase finally said to Mitch.

"She's gone?" he guessed.

"Dropped her knowledge and then went to harass someone else," Chase said. "You feel better?"

"I don't know how we got from salves to me moving to Iowa, but, yeah, I guess I do."

"So I need to pack your stuff and haul it up to Iowa?" Owen asked.

"Maybe," Mitch said, feeling a warmth in his chest. "I need to talk to Paige."

"Okay, good luck," Owen told him. "But, in all seriousness, Ellie has a point. When you find the girl that makes you feel *different*. Different from the other girls but also like you're a different person, better than you were before, then she's worth a U-Haul and a change-of-address form at the post office."

Mitch felt his smile spreading. "Yeah. You've got a point."

He and Paige hadn't been together enough for him to *be* different, but he thought maybe he *could be*.

"I'm jealous," Chase said. "Bailey and I can't really do the change-of-address-U-Haul thing. I mean, she could move to DC, I suppose, but she's happiest down here on the bayou, and I'm only in DC for a couple of years before I'll hopefully be heading back down here anyway."

Mitch grinned. His friend had already decided he wanted to be back closer to Autre. "You think you can do the long-distance thing?" he asked.

Chase paused, and again Mitch imagined he had located Bailey across the room. "Yeah," he said, his voice softer. "Fuck, yeah. We'll get together as much as we can, and the future together is worth however hard it is now."

"And with the way you two are when you're together, it's probably safer if the two of you are mostly together on Zoom or FaceTime," Mitch teased.

Just the other night, they'd disappeared down to the docks for some alone time and come back dripping wet because they'd fallen into the bayou. Bailey was definitely accident prone and she took Chase right down with her.

Chase chuckled. "Good thing I'm going to medical school, huh?"

Mitch laughed. "For sure."

"Okay, so go tell your girl that you're going to need to buy some warmer clothes, and I'm going to go try not to get my nose broken under the mistletoe."

Laughing, they disconnected. Mitch got out of the car and looked up at the light shining in the window of Paige's apartment over the yoga studio.

Here went nothing.

Seven

Man, she was in so much trouble.

She wanted him to stick around. A lot.

The words had just hung in the air between them after she'd said them and then he'd winked at her and left before she could emphasize, "for the *next couple of days.*"

Not that she'd rushed to say that.

It wasn't like she thought there was a chance he might stay more than that.

He lived in Louisiana. He worked in Louisiana. His entire family—which was, evidently, quite large—was in Louisiana.

Plus she did *not* want him to stay. Not like *stay* stay. She was the one who got itchy when a guy wanted to go out two days in a row. Of course, around here, two dates two days in a row meant they were going to discuss honeymoon destinations.

So, no, she did not want Mitch to stay any longer. The story about him and Tori would only hold up so long anyway.

But then he walked into her apartment.

Just let himself in as if he belonged there. Shrugged out of his coat—well, Max's coat—tossed it on the chair as if that was where he always tossed his coat when he came home and stalked toward her.

Her heart started pounding. His nose was a little red from the cold but otherwise, he looked very hot. She realized she'd been imagining him with a tool belt on, even though she'd known he hadn't used a tool belt, while confidently fixing anything and everything anyone threw at him. Smiling and being charming the whole time he did it. Saving the damned Apple Festival that she honestly hadn't cared much about since she was a teenager and she and her friends would go and hope to get caught under the mistletoe.

Now she dodged that damned weed like it was poison ivy.

But the idea that Mitch had fixed the power in the town square, and everyone would know he was the big savior... like Santa, albeit a few weeks late, or maybe like the Grinch when he came blazing into town with all the decorations and gifts after finding his Christmas spirit...made tingles spread through her body. And made her wish for mistletoe.

Though the look on his face at the moment made her pretty sure she wasn't going to need it.

"Hi, how did it—" she started.

He cupped the back of her head and brought her in for a kiss. A very hot, deep, wet, backing-her-up-against-the-wall kiss.

Merry Late Christmas indeed.

She wrapped herself around him and gave a little hop to help when he scooped his hands under her ass and picked her up. He set her on the countertop next to the stove. Where she'd been stirring chocolate and marshmallow fluff together for fudge.

Shit.

She pulled back from him, breathing hard. "Welcome back."

He grinned. "Take your clothes off."

"In five minutes," she said, pushing him back and sliding to the floor.

"Now," he insisted, catching the hem of her top and slipping his hands up underneath it to her stomach as she turned to face the stove.

"I can't let this burn," she said, her inner muscles clenching hard as he dragged his palm back and forth over her stomach.

"You don't have to cook for me." He put his mouth against her neck, rubbing his beard up and down the sensitive skin.

Goose bumps broke out over her whole body making her wiggle against him. And the very prominent erection pressing into her back. She wiggled again just for good measure.

He gave a low growl. "Keep doing that and I'm tossing that whole pot in the sink, and you can just angry fuck me over it."

Her shiver was stronger this time and she sighed. He surprised her with the dirty talk and it always had a strong, immediate effect on her body.

"We need this fudge," she told him. But she had to concentrate on the stirring as his hands moved up to cup her breast.

She hadn't put her bra back on, and he teased the bare nipple making her whimper softly.

"Don't need anything but you," he said gruffly against her ear, tugging on the hard tip.

"We need it for bribery," she said, her eyes sliding closed as she gave the bubbling chocolate a half-assed stir.

"Who are we bribing?"

"Drew Ryan."

"Why does Drew need to be bribed?"

"Because he knows that you're not Tori's fiancé," she explained. "We need to ask him to play along with our story when he's out and about at the festival and hears about the fix-it guy who saved the day."

"And he won't just do it because he's a nice guy?"

"Well, the fudge won't hurt."

Mitch slipped the hand not tormenting her breast into the front of her pants. She also still did not have panties on. His finger slid over her clit making fire lick down her legs and her have to grip the counter with her free hand.

"I wouldn't have pegged you for a fudge maker," he said. "You're pretty sugar-free, gluten-free healthy."

She nodded. "I know. I'm an enigma. I happen to make the best damned fudge you've ever tasted. I started making it before I became a full 'health nut' as my father calls it. So now people beg me for it and what can I say, I'm flattered, so I give in."

Or she said something like that. There was no way she could have repeated any of it. Mitch's finger was circling her clit in lazy loops, and her whole body was melting just like the blob of marshmallow fluff in the pot.

"How much longer?" he asked, sliding his finger lower and teasing her opening.

Her knees wobbled slightly, and she had to take a second before cracking one eye—not realizing her eyes were shut—and peeking at the timer. "Just another minute."

He slid his finger into her and she gasped, clutching the counter.

"Stir, Paige," he said softly, moving his finger in and out.

"You're so mean," she said, practically whispering.

"You want me to stop?" he asked, sliding deeper. "Really?"

"No. God, no." She stirred a little faster and focused on *not* coming.

But damn, he was so good at this. She couldn't remember the last time she'd been with a guy who got her going the way he did.

She was never going to be able to make fudge without thinking of this.

The timer went off, the beeping the best sound she'd ever heard.

"I have to move," she said, picking the pot up from the burner.

He did remove his hands from her body, which she definitely regretted, but as she poured the liquid fudge from the pot into the rectangular pan to set, she heard the rustle of clothes and glanced over her shoulder to find him toeing his boots off and shrugging out of his shirt.

She stopped and stared. *Yes.* God, she loved this man naked.

Something sharp stung her foot and she jumped, looking to

find that fudge was dripping from the spoon in her hand onto her foot.

Dammit!

She quickly dumped the pot and spoon in the sink and checked the cake pan. The fudge was spread evenly, and she, somehow, hadn't burned it. She carried it to the fridge and slid it onto the lowest shelf. Then she turned to Mitch, pulling her shirt up and over her head.

"Anyone else coming over?" he asked, his hot gaze on her breasts and his hands on his fly.

"Grandpa's been here and gone."

"That's great news."

She watched him unzip and shove his jeans to the floor, kicking them off. Behind the plain black boxers, he was huge and hard. And she was suddenly hotter than she'd ever been.

She slipped out of her yoga pants leaving them in the middle of the kitchen floor. Naked, she padded to him.

"Now what?" she asked, stopping right in front of him and looking up at him.

"You'll do anything I want?" he asked, his voice rough and his eyes hot.

"Definitely."

"How hot is the fudge?"

Her eyes widened. "Hot. Too hot for smearing on body parts," she said, reading his mind.

One side of his mouth curled. "Damn."

"But," she said, "I have some fudge we could heat up a little."

"You have some already made?" he asked. "Why was I waiting for you to stir that up?"

"The fudge I've already got is for you." She felt her cheeks get a little pink. She was *shy* about this? She was buck naked at the moment, and he'd done a lot of *intimate* things to her already, but admitting she'd made him fudge made her blush?

"You made me fudge?"

Dammit. He looked pleased by that. He was so going to get

the wrong idea. Especially when she told him the whole story. She sighed. "Yeah. I made it around Christmas. I was going to mail it to you but then... I changed my mind."

"You were going to *send* me fudge for Christmas?" he asked, his grin growing. He lifted a hand to her cheek.

"Yes. But then I realized that you'd think it meant I liked you and was thinking about you," she said with an eye roll.

"Oh, sweetheart," he said, his voice dropping and that drawl becoming more pronounced. "I *know* you like me and have been thinking of me."

He was cocky. A little. Not overly. Not obnoxiously. But enough to be... hot. She did like confident men. "Well, you can *not* think that the fact that it's chipotle fudge means *anything*," she said.

His grin definitely grew with that. "You made me spicy fudge?"

"Spicy and sweet go together really well."

He nodded, his grin turning into an almost smirk. "They sure do."

"But it was just something I wanted to try, and since you eat all that crazy spicy food I thought you were someone I could send it to."

"But then you realized that I'd think it meant you liked me."

She blew out a breath. "Yeah."

"Do you normally make chipotle fudge?"

"No."

"Huh."

"You're thinking it, aren't you?"

"That you like me? Yeah, I'm thinking it."

"Well, if you're going to be all smug about it, I'm not going to melt it down and coat your cock with it so I can lick it off."

His smile dropped and his eyes blazed. "Oh yes you fucking are."

"What if the chili powder in it burns you?"

"I can handle that," he told her. "For sure."

The powder, especially mixed in with all the other ingredients, probably wasn't much of a risk. There was just enough in the fudge to give it some kick.

"That's pretty sensitive skin," she pointed out anyway.

"True. Guess you'll have to lick fast."

"And thoroughly," she agreed.

"Definitely."

"But I don't want to use it all up. I want you take some of it back to Louisiana with you." She gave him a grin that she was sure looked very please-fuck-me. At least that's what she was thinking. "And think of me... and what we're about to do... while you eat it."

"Yeah, we need to talk about me thinking about you from Louisiana," he said.

Oooh, that sounded like he maybe wanted to take their texting to sexting. Or maybe even phone sex. Or the Zoom sex he'd mentioned earlier. She was on board.

"Later. We can talk and... do a lot of other things... *later*." She ran her hand down his abs and stroked his cock through his boxers. "But we have other things to do right now."

She turned and reached to grab the container of spicy fudge from the counter. She was glad she'd mentioned it. She wasn't going to. She wasn't going to confess that he'd made her do something special and different. But somehow it felt right to admit that now.

Then she took his hand and led him down the hallway to her bedroom.

She pushed him toward the bed and shut the door behind her. No one else was coming over. Probably. Okay, there was a 5 percent chance that someone else would stop by. At least this way she'd hear them unlock the front door and could stash him in her closet before whoever it was made it down the hall.

If she heard them.

She had some plans here that just might end up being kind of noisy.

Mitch sitting on the edge of her bed, his hot, hard, tanned body and black boxers against the multicolored quilt and pillows was about the sexiest thing she'd ever seen. He looked out of place on the squares covered with stitched flowers and swirls. Her pillows were encased in different pillowcases as well. Something that, for some reason, drove her mom crazy. They were a mismatched bunch from different sheet sets. A couple had come from childhood sets, a couple from her grandmother, and she had no idea where the purple one had come from. But why did every-thing always have to match? Why did things have to go a certain way all the time? Why did there have to be a *plan* for every damned thing including matching sheets?

She took a deep breath. That didn't matter. At least not at this moment. Mitch looked out of place and she *loved* that. He didn't match and that was awesome. He wasn't like the guys here. He wasn't from here. Her mother didn't know his mother and grand-mother and every aunt and cousin. *She* didn't know his mother. Nor would she.

This was perfect.

She pulled the top off the fudge container and took a piece out. Then she tossed the box on top of her dresser and walked toward Mitch.

He opened his knees, welcoming her between them, his hands going to her butt.

She lifted the fudge and took a bite, then offered it to him. He bit into it, his eyes locked on hers.

The candy was incredibly sweet. She didn't eat much white sugar and very, very few candies. But she was definitely happy to make an exception here. The chili powder kept it from being too much as the chocolate melted on her tongue and the spiciness gave her a little tingle.

Mitch's fingers curled into her butt as he let the fudge melt in his mouth as well. Paige shifted to put a knee on the mattress next to him, pressing her body against his. She lowered her mouth, meeting his lips in a chocolatey, sweet and spicy kiss. This was by far her favorite way to eat fudge.

Except...

The piece of candy had grown a little sticky as she held it. She put it in her other hand and lifted her chocolatey fingertips to her nipple. She coated it in chocolate and then lifted her head from the kiss.

Mitch's gaze immediately found her sticky nipple and his lips followed.

He took the tip in his mouth, swirling his tongue around it, then sucking.

Her fingers gripped his head as she sighed. God, this was so good. Sex had never been like this before. No one had ever turned her on like this man. No one had ever known how to touch her, how to talk to her, the way he did.

"My turn," she said breathlessly, pushing him back.

She went to her knees in front of him, pulling one side of his boxers down. She still held the piece of fudge in her other hand, so needed his help—which he gladly gave—to slide his boxers down. She shifted out of the way so he could get them off his feet, but her gaze and her hand, immediately went to the impressive cock he exposed.

"You have to tell me if this hurts you," she said, looking up at him from beneath her lashes as she moved the fudge from her fingertips to her full palm. She closed her fist around it, letting it get melty.

"Oh babe, give me some good hurt," he said, his hand going to her head.

She was so glad he wasn't going to try to talk her out of this or even say something like *you don't have to do this*. She *did* have to do this. She *needed* to. She wanted him to get hard as soon as he opened that box of fudge when he was home.

Paige reached for him with her sticky hand and ran it up and down his hard length, leaving a chocolatey mess behind.

He hissed out a breath as she touched him, rubbing and squeezing, his fingers tightened against her scalp.

Then she leaned in and put her tongue to work cleaning up the mess. She licked and sucked until he was gripping her hair and breathing raggedly.

"Paige. Fuck. God. Sweetheart."

He could only manage single words it seemed, and she felt a definite surge of power knowing she was making him lose the ability to speak.

She took him deep and felt his whole body stiffen.

"No. Not like this."

Suddenly she found herself hauled to her feet, swung around, and tossed onto the mattress.

He immediately crawled up her body. He took her mouth in a deep, searing kiss and she arched into him, seeking full-body contact and heat. She needed all of his hardness against all of her softness.

He drove his fingers into her hair, holding her head still as he kissed her, his tongue stroking deep and amazingly making her clit ache as if he were licking it. She gripped his shoulders, wrapping her legs around him.

His cock pressed against her, hot and heavy and she whimpered. "Please, Mitch."

"Anything you want."

"You. Just you. All of you. Please."

"I don't know if I can take you slow, sweetheart." He moved his mouth along her jaw. "I'm trying to get some control here."

"No. Not slow." She tried to shake her head, but he still held her. She looked up at him. "Hard. Please."

He blew out a breath. "The first time... we got a little wild. But this time, I've been thinking about you, *waiting* for you, for a long time now. This might be... really hard."

When he'd told her before that he hadn't been with anyone else it had sent a shot of adrenaline through her that had felt a lot like panic. This was too intense, too fast, too much. She didn't want to be totally absorbed in someone. She didn't want someone who would be totally absorbed in her.

But now when he said it, she felt a surge of a different kind. *Mine.*

She had *never* felt that way about another person. She didn't feel that way about a single possession, her apartment, or her hometown. She didn't even feel it when she looked at her yoga studio or thought about the business she'd created. She felt it about her cats in some cases. Technically they were all available for adoption, but she kept *her* cats, the ones she just felt needed *her* and no one else, in another room when people came to look to adopt.

But in that moment, with Mitch, with him telling her that he'd been *waiting* on her, she felt it.

Mine. She wanted him to be hers.

She was so screwed.

"Yes," she said softly. She pressed one heel into his ass, but she moved her hands to hold his face. "Hard. Deep. Take me, Mitch."

His jaw tensed as he stared into her eyes for a long moment. Then he gave her a nod. "Glad we're on that same page."

She had a feeling the page they were on was not the fuck-me-hard page. It was more than that. Deeper. More serious.

But it didn't make her stomach tighten with trepidation. It made her whole body tighten with anticipation.

"Condom," he said, shifting slightly. "Dammit. They're in the other room."

She shook her head and pointed at her bedside table. "In there."

She had condoms in her bedside table. She rarely used them in here. Mostly she just grabbed them and stuffed them in her purse if she was going out with someone that she might want to use one with. She, frustratingly, couldn't keep them in the bathroom where her mother might see them. Not that she was embarrassed that her mom knew she had sex. It was that her mom would want to know who the guy was and how serious it was and did he have a good job and did he like meatloaf.

She just couldn't handle all of that, so she hid her condoms. Like a teenager sneaking around. Ugh, she hated that.

But Mitch didn't seem too annoyed by the idea that she had, and had needed, condoms in her bedside table. He shifted and reached, grabbing them out of the drawer and tossing about five on the quilt next to them.

His eyes locked on hers as he pushed up to kneel between her thighs, and rolled a condom on.

Damn, that was hot.

Then he lowered himself on top of her again and kissed her.

It was the sexiest, sweetest kiss of her life.

She wasn't sure what was different about it. It was still lips and tongues. But there was more there now.

Lord, just please don't let him propose.

Then as he lifted her leg a little higher and pressed forward, sliding into her, and her neck arched, her head pressing back into the mattress with the sheer delicious bliss of it, she added, *And don't let* me *propose to* him.

Mitch slid in deep and then paused.

She tightened around him and he groaned.

"Hard," she whispered.

"Okay." He pulled in a breath. "Hang on."

She grinned. "You break my bed, you have to fix it."

"Can do."

She didn't know if he was referring to breaking her bed or fixing it, but she knew he could do both.

Mitch shifted to brace his arm on the mattress next to her ear. The other gripped her thigh, lifting it, and spreading her a little wider.

And then he went hard. Braced above her, he was able to thrust deep and hard, and her headboard began banging against the wall just slightly louder than her gasps and cries of, "Oh,

Mitch!" and "Yes!" and his growls and, "Fuck, yeahs" and "God, you're amazing."

Her hand gripped his shoulder while the other grabbed on to the quilt under her. But she couldn't do much more than lay there and take it. And she loved every second of that.

She was not the submissive type. At all. But something about letting Mitch do any dirty thing he wanted to made her hot and needy.

And all his.

Did he ever think *mine* about her? Surely not. They barely knew one another. She had no idea why *she* was thinking those things. There was no way he was thinking them too.

"Paige. Baby. Honey." He was panting as he thrust.

She arched closer. "Yes. Yes. Yes."

And then she was coming. Hard. The waves of pleasure washing through her took her breath away, and for just a second she thought *I can't live without this.*

Mitch's pace picked up, his body tensing, and he was coming, her name a long groan as he let go.

He held himself up from her for several seconds as they both breathed hard. Then he leaned down and kissed her. This was soft, but still as hot as the hungry ones from before. His lips clung to hers for a moment, then he kissed his way along her jaw and down her neck to her shoulder, before rolling to his side and bringing her nearly boneless body up against his until she was half draped over him.

"Holy. Shit," he said, breathing out in a very satisfied way.

She smiled against his chest. "Ditto."

It had been good. So good. Better than the first time they'd been together last summer.

But, of course, she could live without it. That had been a crazy thought. It was just sex. *Really good* sex, but still. It wasn't like it was oxygen or water.

But as he shifted and settled more fully into her mattress, his hand possessively splayed over her ass, she had a twinge of *I don't want him to leave* that was very concerning.

A huge yawn hit her just then, and she stretched as she pulled in the long, deep breath before settling against him again.

She was definitely going to need to think about all of her crazy thoughts and feelings about this guy and figure out what the hell was wrong with her and how to get over it.

Mitch kissed the top of her head and she smiled and sighed.

She'd figure out how to get over it—*him*—tomorrow.

Or maybe the day after that.

Eight

He woke her up twice during the night. Normally that alone would have been enough for her to put a lot of distance between them immediately. Not having anyone dictating or interrupting her routines and schedules was one very big pro of being single.

But Mitch really made the waking up worthwhile.

Until he started talking after the second wake-up call via orgasm.

It had been going so well too. His hot mouth. His hot hands. His hot... everything else. Who cared about sleep when you had a big, hot, dirty-talking, sexy, sweet Cajun in your bed?

No one, that was who.

But big, hot, dirty-talking, sexy, sweet, *chatty* Cajuns were another thing.

"I was thinkin'," he said, his drawl more pronounced in the dark, and after his second orgasm.

"Uh-oh," Paige said. Out loud. Sincerely.

He gave her butt a squeeze. "I'm serious."

"Exactly why I said *uh-oh*." She shifted and propped up on her elbow. The room wasn't pitch black. Lights from the street outside filtered in through the gauzy curtains, and she still had twinkle lights up around the window.

He definitely looked serious. Hot. Sexy as hell. And serious.

She sighed. "Is there any chance you've been thinking about asking how I feel about being tied up in bed or nipple clamps or something?"

He cleared his throat, and she felt his hand tighten on her butt. But he shook his head. Unfortunately.

"I'm pretty sure you're a solid don't-you-fucking-dare-tie-me-up girl," he said.

She nodded. "You wouldn't be wrong." She never wanted to give up that much control. To anyone.

But nipple clamps might be something else...

"I want to stay."

Four words. No preamble. No easing into it. Just *I want to stay.*

And her heart flipped over. Then plummeted.

"Stay? Like here in bed rather than going to the festival? Or for a couple extra days? Or..."

"For good."

Dammit. She sighed and shifted farther away. For a second his arm tightened around her as if wanting to hold her in place, but then he relaxed and let her slip out from his arm. She pushed herself up to sitting and leaned over to grab her sweatshirt off the floor. The first garment she touched, however, was his t-shirt. She pulled it on anyway. She just needed to be covered.

Then she faced him.

He had shifted so he was propped up against her headboard. The sheet covered him from the waist down, but not his shoulders, chest, or abs.

Dammit. *Willpower. You have to have willpower.*

"So," she started, folding her hands in her lap and resting her elbows on her thighs, "that's crazy."

He nodded. "I know it seems that way."

"It doesn't just *seem* that way, Mitch," she said. "It *is* crazy.

People don't just spend a couple of days together and then move a thousand miles from home to be together."

"People in my family do stuff like that all the time," he said, lifting a shoulder.

"Even more reason to stay far away from you and your family," she muttered.

"Tori's doing it."

Paige shook her head. "She knew Josh longer than we've known each other."

"Not that much."

"Well, I'm not Tori." She frowned.

He chuckled. Actually *chuckled* at that.

But it was true. Tori was fine with falling in love and making a long-term commitment. Paige was... not.

"What?" she asked.

"So you like your life the way it is? Your family drives you crazy being in your business all the time. The town drives you crazy being in your business all the time. You're judged for everything you do from your work to how you spend your free time to what you eat."

Paige opened her mouth to reply. But then she snapped it shut. Well... fuck. He was right, of course. How did he know all of that? He'd just figured it all out?

"So the last thing I want," she said, grabbing on to her argument. "Is *another* person in my business."

"I don't want to tell you what to eat or what job you should do."

"But you want to change how I live."

"No... I..." He frowned. "That's not what I'm trying to do."

"But it's what would happen. *Any* relationship changes my life, brings one more person in that needs to be a part of decisions and choices from what I do in the evening after work to how I spend my birthday. I've been *considerate* of the men who want to date me by saying no to anything more than a casual fling or hookup."

He scowled at that. "It's been *considerate* of you to not spend their birthdays with them, to not want to hang out with them and go to the festival or movies together?"

She threw up her hands. "Yes! If I don't want to spend every moment with them or have their opinions or advice on how I'm living my life, then it's *nice* of me to not lead them on thinking that I *do* want those things."

"That's not—"

"And I'd *especially* feel obligated to share my life with someone who would have moved *his* entire life a thousand miles just to be with me. I couldn't just let you sit at home by yourself here without feeling guilty. You wouldn't know anyone else here or have anything else to do."

"I'm not asking..." He shoved his hand through his hair.

She lifted a brow. "Then what are you asking?"

"For you to give this a chance. A *real* chance. To honestly see if this could be something."

"Right. To date you. Seriously. Exclusively. To go to movies and spend my birthday with you."

"*Yes,*" he finally said, exasperated. "Yes. I want to be with you. A lot. I want to see what this could be if I lived here, or close enough, to see you more often. I want to get to know you. So, yes, Paige, I want to move here and see you every single day and be a part of your life."

Her stomach flipped at his words. But she wasn't sure if it was dread... or temptation.

"I've been proposed to four times."

He paused, his hand partway through his hair again. It dropped as he stared at her. "What?"

She nodded. "I've been proposed to four times. Twice by the same guy, so three guys. But four proposals."

He looked completely confused. "You're twenty-two."

"Yeah. The first time was right after my high school graduation."

"Um... wow."

"And I said yes to that one."

He scowled. "You've been *engaged*? Already?"

"Yep. Guy I'd known my whole life. My mom's best friend's son." She shrugged, her chest aching the way it always did when she thought of Garrett. He had been such a great guy. Still was a great guy. And she'd not only broken his heart and ended their lifelong friendship, but she'd broken his mom's heart and the heart of everyone in her family.

They would have been a little frustrated or even mad if she hadn't dated him at all, but nothing like the hurt and disappointment after she'd ended the engagement.

Now she really tried with everything in her not to break hearts. Any hearts.

Her mom didn't like her yoga studio or cat collection, but Paige was upfront about those being what she wanted, so Dee was just frustrated... and worried... but not *heartbroken* about those choices.

"Jesus." Mitch blew out a breath. "What happened?"

She shrugged. "We turned sixteen and our moms had always said they wished we'd date. So we did. And then... it's how things go here. You date. You get engaged. You get married. You get jobs. You have kids."

"But..." Mitch frowned. "You didn't."

She shook her head. "I was trying on wedding dresses. My mom was all teary-eyed about it. Amanda was so excited. Everyone was so happy. Except the girl in the mirror. I realized I was doing it for them and that I didn't want to get married. Not at age nineteen for sure. But not to Garrett any time. So I took the dress off, told them it was over, walked out, broke up with him, and... they've never fully forgiven me."

Mitch was just staring at her. "And..." He shook his head. "The other two?"

"Adam was the next one. We had some chemistry—I mean, I didn't hate kissing him or anything. And neither of us were planning to go off to college so I guess he figured why not."

"That is..." Mitch shook his head. "Wow."

"He was the one that proposed twice. After his dad passed away and he took over the farm completely just last spring, he asked me again."

"Had you been dating then?"

"Nope."

Mitch shook his head again. "And the other one?"

"Similar thing. Guy I've known forever who settled down here and getting married is the next thing on his to-do list. He looked around, saw a girl who seemed to be in a similar place, took me out to dinner a couple times, had some not-terrible sex, and then popped the question."

"You slept with them?" he asked with a frown.

"Not Adam," she said. "The one who asked twice. Garrett, the one I said yes to, sure. And the other one..." She shrugged. "Yeah."

Mitch seemed to be gritting his teeth. "You didn't explain the hookup-only rule to him?"

"Actually, I did." She leaned in. "But he didn't listen. Because that's not what he wanted to hear."

Just like *he* wasn't listening. She knew that he got the point.

"Everyone here is just marriage crazy?" he asked.

She shrugged. "It's just... what you do. It's just the natural progression. Or a bad habit. Or a contagious disease. Or something."

He snorted.

"You think I'm kidding? My *three* best friends from high school are already married."

"And they're all your age?"

She nodded. "And they all married their prom dates."

His eyes widened. "Prom is like a giant mass engagement event here or something?"

"It's serious. No one here believes in just... fucking around. Having fun. Doing anything... temporary. Everything is long term and about futures." She sighed. "One of my friends married the only guy she ever *kissed*. They started 'dating' when they were ten. Another married the guy who asked her to prom. I mean, they had *a little bit* of an excuse. She got pregnant prom night."

Mitch snorted again. "Prom is trouble around here."

"Oh, for sure. But they're still together and have *two more* kids." She rolled her eyes. "And *another* friend, the one I had big hopes for, left her high school boyfriend behind to go off to college, but she only lasted a semester before she was back here, going to school in Dubuque, and planning their wedding."

"Wow." Mitch nodded. "Okay, so there's a lot of pressure."

"Oh, and that's not even my family," she said. "My grandparents eloped when they were seventeen. My parents were childhood sweethearts. My sister married her high school boyfriend and had two kids by the time she was twenty-four and she wants two more."

"Josie didn't marry her high school boyfriend," Mitch pointed out.

"Only because she didn't have one. Sure, she's marrying an outsider, but she's always been a romantic, wanting to settle down and the whole thing. And they're living in a house that's been in my family for five generations. She's working a job in a business that's been a staple in this town for fifty years. She's seeing the same people she always sees. She sees my family *all the time*."

"She must like it." Mitch was frowning.

"She does." Paige didn't doubt that for a minute, and she didn't begrudge her sisters their happiness. It was just that their lives made *her* feel restless and itchy.

"So what do *you* want?" he asked.

She took a breath. "It's going to sound selfish." Her oldest sister had flat-out told her it was selfish as a matter of fact.

"Hit me," he said, making a *come on* motion.

"A Year of Aloneness."

He studied her, then one corner of his mouth curled. "A Year of Aloneness?"

She nodded. "I want to go to Colorado and have a Year of

Aloneness. I want to live alone in a new place where it's not weird to be a yoga-doing, cat collecting, vegetarian. Where no one has known me for even six months not to mention since I was born. And where *no one* will propose to me."

Mitch didn't say anything for a long moment. "For a year, huh?"

"At least." She could go a hell of a lot longer than a year not being proposed to. Or even just not being considered a weird failure. But a year seemed like a great starting point.

"And when does this year begin?"

"When I have enough money saved up."

"Why Colorado?"

"Steamboat Springs is a gorgeous place with a happy, healthy population. They have hot springs and tourists. Seems like a good place to have a yoga studio. And while I save up money, I'm getting my massage therapy license too. Yoga and massages seem to go with hot springs and gorgeous walking trails with stunning mountain views, don't you think?"

"I guess I've never given hot springs and yoga a lot of thought," Mitch said. "But I'll take your word for it."

She shrugged. "I actually hope I can just work for someone else. That would be easier. No roots."

"You're against roots?"

"I've got so many roots right now that I can barely pick my feet up." She sighed. "I'd like to be rootless for a while."

"For a year."

She tipped her head. He was hung up on that it seemed. "*At least*," she added.

"Right." He seemed to be thinking that over.

Paige frowned. "Told you that it sounded selfish."

"It doesn't," he denied. "You have... a lot here."

"I do."

He shifted, sitting up a little straighter. "So it's not marriage you're against. Just the importance your family has put on it."

She frowned, wondering why he cared so much how she felt

about marriage. She swore to God, if he proposed to her, she'd throw him out in the snow. Without Max's coat.

Maybe without his pants.

"It's the idea that I'm weird or failing if I don't have the marriage and family and mortgage thing."

"So that's what you want to get away from. Their expectations and pressures."

"Yes."

He sat forward. "Come to Louisiana."

Her heart flipped in her chest. "What?"

He'd better not be proposing. Though asking her to come to Louisiana was *not* just a movie date.

"For the wedding. Josh and Tori's," he added.

She breathed out. But she couldn't deny there was a tiny twinge of disappointment. "Oh. Yeah, I could—"

"Then stay."

She felt her mouth drop open.

"Shake it up. Tell your family you're going to do your own thing. In Louisiana. They won't have a front row for your life there. They won't even know what you're doing, so they can't judge it."

That was crazy.

And it sounded nice.

"Just move to Louisiana?"

"Yep. I can give you a place to live. Free by the way." He gave her a little wink. "And a job. You can save up money there just as easy as you can here. Maybe easier. No rent. No paying business overhead."

She also sat forward. "I'm guessing the place to live would be with you?"

"In my house," he said with a nod. "But it's got four bedrooms. There's another guy living there too. Works for our family business. He's our veterinarian."

Her own bedroom. But in his house. Uh-huh. "What's the job?"

"Otter yoga."

Her eyebrows rose. "Um... what?"

He chuckled. "I mean, you can do more than that. But there are no yoga studios in Autre."

"Hmm..." She quirked an eyebrow. "Otters?"

He grinned. "We have otters. A whole family of them. We've decided to start an otter encounter as a part of the Boys of the Bayou business. People can come and interact with the otters, feed them, play with them. Seems like a girl who is used to doing yoga with cats, could figure something out with otters too."

That sounded fun, actually. Otters were adorable.

"We have alligators too. Turtles. Lizards."

"Yoga with *alligators*?"

"Maybe the babies?"

She laughed.

"And we're getting a llama. Tori is taking one back with us. Maybe two. Knowing Tori, actually, probably three."

"From Drew and Dallas Ryan?"

"Yep."

"They're alpacas, actually."

"Right. Alpacas."

Alpaca yoga. Otter yoga. Seeing Mitch every day. Hmmm...

"My family would assume that we'd run off and, of course, gotten married," she said.

"And when we don't, that will *really* make them wonder," Mitch said. "They'll just have to guess about what the hell is going on." He leaned closer. "Admit it, that could be kind of fun."

It could be.

A chance to have a relationship without any outside influences? To spend time with a guy and actually see what could happen without anyone else's hopes getting up? A chance to really date someone without worrying about breaking her mom's heart if it didn't work out?

"You *promise* you're not going to propose?" she asked.

"I think I can resist." He gave her a half grin.

That wasn't an *I promise*, but she smiled back.

"Living with you and some other guy isn't really *aloneness*," she pointed out.

"No." He nodded. "There's not a lot of space or alone time in my life, I'll admit."

Yeah, see that was a red flag. She didn't want to trade one crazy big family for another.

"But you're still saving up for the Year of Aloneness, right?" he asked.

"Right." She was probably six months away, honestly. She wanted to have enough to pay rent for at least part of the year in Colorado without worrying about her job situation.

"So come do that in Autre. Away from the proposals that keep happening up here." He actually frowned slightly at that.

She grinned. Was he jealous? She hated herself for liking that idea.

"You worried they might wear me down and I'll finally say yes to one just to shut everyone up?"

His frowned deepened. "Let's just say I don't hate the idea of you being away from all the marriage-minded guys that seem to populate this little town."

Paige laughed lightly. "That should be a huge reason *not* to come to Louisiana, you know."

He reached out and snagged her wrist, tugging her up the bed. She went. Willingly.

He rolled her under him and kissed her long and deep. When he lifted his head, he said, "Come to Louisiana and be my friend with benefits for a few months."

"That's it? That's all you want?"

"I want you to have what *you* want," he said, his eyes sincere.

A little bit of her resolve melted. She actually felt it turn to liquid and slip away.

"And I do want men to stop proposing to you," he added. "Louisiana seems like a good place for you to land temporarily."

She smiled and ran a hand up the side of his face. "You're very tempting."

He pressed his cock against her hip and she felt her body heat instantly. "I promise the benefits will be nice."

"Your other roommate is a heavy sleeper?" she teased.

"He can get his ass out if he doesn't like it," Mitch said gruffly, dragging his jaw along hers.

She shivered and arched closer.

A place to land temporarily. A little adventure. A chance to save up the money she needed but be out from under the magnifying glass of Appleby. Well, her family in particular. The whole town seemed to think that marriage and family were the ultimate goals, but her family was particularly obsessed.

Her Year of Aloneness was still the plan, but she couldn't afford to do it yet, and the idea of spending another six months here did give her a little *ugh* feeling.

And otter yoga? Come on. That sounded really cool.

"How about I come for Tori and Josh's wedding and we see how it goes?" she asked.

He shook his head, but he was smiling. "Can't even commit to six months?"

"Six months is a *long* time."

"Okay... six days. Promise six days when you come to the wedding. I want to really show you the bayou." He lowered his head and kissed her neck, then dragged his mouth up the sensitive skin to her ear. "And everything you can have if you stay there."

She arched into him, unable to help it. The *stay there* gave her pause. But he meant for six months. That wasn't too long. Not long enough to mess up any plans, anyway. Probably.

Then he dragged his mouth down her neck, past her shoulder, to her breast. He pushed his shirt up and took her nipple in his mouth, and all she could think was *I'll give you six of whatever you want, Mitch Landry.*

Nine

Paige rolled over and eyed her clock. Then sat straight upright. Nine a.m.?

Nine? How had she slept till nine? She had yoga...

Wait, no, she didn't. It was the first day of the festival and everything else in town shut down.

She started to lay back down. Why was she so tired though?

Then sat straight up again.

Mitch.

She was tired because of Mitch. The sex. The *talking*. The sex. And geez, the *talking*.

She looked around. Where was he? His side of the bed was still rumpled, but it was cold when she touched the sheets, and there wasn't a sound in her apartment.

Had he actually snuck out and *left*?

Had he realized that everything he said last night about her going to Louisiana for a few months was batshit crazy and gotten out before she woke up and he found himself with a live-in girlfriend he barely knew? And her twenty-three cats?

Hmm... the cats. She was going to have to figure something out with the cats. She'd thought she had a few months before she moved to Colorado and had been figuring out a way to take them with her...

She shook her head. She needed to focus. She didn't need to figure out what to do with her cats when she went to Louisiana if Mitch had snuck out and taken off for Louisiana without her.

That would be such a good thing.

So why did she feel really disappointed?

Paige threw back the sheets and got out of bed. She was *not* disappointed. The whole conversation had come on the heels of major orgasm endorphins in the middle of the night. No rational life decisions should be made in that circumstance.

But two minutes later, she did at least admit to herself that she was looking for a note from him.

He couldn't even leave a note?

She reached for her phone, thinking maybe there was at least a text. Maybe he'd waited until he was safely driving through Oklahoma...

Her phone rang just then.

It was her sister's number.

"Hello?"

"Good morning," Josie greeted brightly.

Paige leaned back against her counter. Josie was a morning person. Paige was not. Paige got up early. But she liked quiet and meditation and slow, gentle stretching first thing. Josie was bright and bubbly and thought the day should be started with caffeine and sugar.

It made the fact that she worked in the local bakery very convenient.

"Morning," Paige said.

Josie was calling her to come help at the bakery. Paige could feel it. She often filled in at Buttered Up. It was a block away and sometimes they needed extra hands. She was happy to do it. Usually. Right now she was feeling very *unbubbly* and sweet this morning.

Which was so stupid. Mitch realizing his suggestion was crazy and getting out of town, thereby keeping her from having to tell him it was crazy and say no in the morning light when she wasn't hopped up on endorphins was a *good* thing.

"You should stop by the bakery this morning," Josie said.

She knew it. "You guys swamped?"

The bakery didn't close completely on festival day, just early. But they opened so people could get breakfast and coffee before hitting the chilly town square. In fact, it was a big business day.

"We are," Josie said. "You should stop by."

"I'm not really hungry." She was grumpy. About a guy. Wow, she needed... something.

"You don't have to eat."

"So what would I do?" Help at the register, probably. Which would at least take her mind off Mitch. Maybe that was good.

"You could just talk."

"Talk?" Paige frowned. "We can talk later."

"I mean to Tori."

Paige froze. Then straightened away from the counter. "Tori?"

"Tori Kramer. She's here with her fiancé. And his cousin. Who is *hot*. You should totally come down here and meet him."

Tori was at Buttered Up? With Josh? And... Mitch?

Paige's heart *thunked* so hard in her chest she actually lifted her hand and pressed it over the spot.

Wow. She was in so much trouble here.

But... *fuck*.

If Tori was there with Josh, then it would be clear that *Mitch* was not her fiancé, and if anyone walked in who thought he was— and that was *very* possible—they were screwed. Linda, Carol, Melanie, Mike, Larry... hell, the whole town...were regulars at the bakery.

As was Paige's mother.

Ugh.

"I'll be right there," she said quickly, heading for her bedroom.

"Awesome," Josie said happily.

Paige stopped. Crap. She'd sounded enthusiastic about getting down there to meet Tori's hot cousin. But... she couldn't deal with her romance-loving sister right now. "See you soon." She disconnected and tossed the phone on the bed and headed for the shower.

Fifteen minutes later, Paige let herself in through the back door of the bakery. That was a friends-with-the-owner privilege that Paige happily used this morning. She couldn't just walk in through the front without checking things out.

She came up short when she found the kitchen full.

"What are you all doing here?"

Whitney and Jane both grinned.

"Packing apple pies up for the booth at the festival."

Every business in town had a booth in the square, including the bakery. Even though everyone had spent the holidays overeating and most of the town stopped in here this morning on their way over there. The stuff at the booth was taken home and saved for when people were in the mood for sweets again. Like in a couple of days.

Jane and Whitney didn't work at the bakery but they were Zoe and Josie's best friends. They had big boxes and tons of packing peanuts in front of them and were filling the boxes with little mason jars. Zoe had started doing cakes and pies in jars and they'd been a big hit. They were especially great for expos and fairs.

Paige focused on Whitney. She and Whitney had also become friends over the past few months. Whitney had been a regular at yoga and a few months back had reached out for a girls' night out. Paige had turned her down the first time but since then they'd gone out a few times.

That first time, she'd had to decline because Tori was in town. With her fiancé. And his hot cousin.

Paige had also spilled about that hot cousin to Whitney over hard ciders at Granny Smith's, the local bar.

She crossed the room, braced her hands on the worktable across from Whitney and narrowed her eyes. "What did you do?"

Whitney's eyes widened. "About what?"

"What did you tell my sister about Tori's fiancé and his hot cousin?" she asked, shooting a glance at Jane.

Jane kept packing her box. But she was clearly fighting a smile.

Shit. They all knew. Paige could tell.

Whitney shrugged. "I just..." Then she blew out a breath. "You should have told me it was a secret."

"You told Josie who Mitch is?"

"I just said that you had a hot night with a guy with a sexy Louisiana accent."

Okay, so that would...

"And I might have said the name Mitch." Whitney bit her bottom lip.

"You totally said the name Mitch," Jane said with a snort.

Paige groaned. "Whit."

"I'm sorry."

"Why are you trying to hide this?" Jane asked.

"Oh, hey!" Josie swept into the kitchen just then from the front of the bakery. She gave Paige a big grin. "They're right out front. He's *very* cute."

Paige shot Jane a glance. Jane met her eyes and gave a nod. Yeah, she got it. She knew Paige's family. She knew Josie best, of course, and Josie's romantic streak was just an adorable part of Josie's adorable personality. When that romantic streak was about her own life. But when it was turned on the people around her and she wanted everyone to fall in love, it wasn't quite as cute.

Jane had experienced that too.

"Have you talked to them?" Paige asked her sister.

"I waited on them," Josie said with a nod. "But it's crazy out there, so we didn't really *talk*."

"Oh, do you guys need help?" Paige asked. Hey, she was here now. She could pitch in. And avoid the table with Tori and Josh and Mitch and whatever they had told everyone about... whatever.

"Nope. Maggie and Cam both came in to help bake this morning," Josie said of Zoe's mom and brother—Whitney's boyfriend. "And Grant and Aiden are out there helping Zoe wait on everyone." Her smile was soft and affectionate as she mentioned her fiancé, Grant, and Zoe's, Aiden.

Well, they really were covered. With all of those people, two of them big guys, there probably wasn't room behind the counter anyway.

And, really, she probably did need to go find out what Mitch had told Tori and Josh about their little lie about Mitch and Tori being engaged. Paige's cover wasn't entirely blown because Josie still, apparently, thought Mitch was Tori's fiancé.

Plus she wanted to see Mitch. She wasn't able to forget the disappointment she'd felt thinking he'd hightailed it back to Louisiana. She liked him more than she'd wanted to admit.

"Go introduce yourself to the cousin," Josie urged. "You and Tori are friends. Just go out and join them."

Okay, so apparently Whitney had slipped about Mitch in front of Jane but not Josie? That was fortunate. She supposed.

And Josie was reading Paige's hesitation as nerves about meeting a new guy. Well, that was better than her guessing that Paige was nervous that Mitch was going to upend all of her carefully laid plans.

"Oh my gosh!"

Paige had to jump back as the swinging door that led to the front of the bakery suddenly swung in, almost whacking her in the face.

"Hey, Kelsey!" Josie greeted Jane's younger sister.

"Hi," she said to everyone collectively. Then she focused on Jane. "Guess what?"

Jane turned and faced her. "What?"

"Look what Matt gave me for my birthday!" Kelsey held up

the little heart-shaped charm hanging from the chain around her neck.

"Oh wow," Josie said, moving in before Jane could. "That's so pretty!"

Kelsey nodded, nearly squealing. "He said that now I can *actually* take his heart with me wherever I go."

Paige caught herself before she rolled her eyes.

Josie, on the other hand, audibly sighed. "That's so romantic."

"Oh wow, Kels, that's awesome," Jane said.

Was it? Maybe. What did Paige know?

"That really is," Whitney agreed.

Okay, so all of the women who were in *actual* relationships thought Matt had done something good here. Fine. The kid was a senior in high school giving another senior in high school a birthday gift after dating for about six months. He was Kelsey's first serious boyfriend. There had probably been some pressure to make it meaningful. Paige probably needed to lighten up.

"His birthday is two days after mine," Kelsey said.

"No way," Whitney said.

Kelsey nodded. "Cute, right?"

They all laughed. "Very cute," Josie agreed. "What did you get him?"

"It's not as good as this," Kelsey said, shaking her head. "I told him I'd play *Warriors of Easton* with him for an entire weekend."

"That *is* good," Jane said. "He loves *Warriors* and always wants you to play but knows you don't really like it. That's sweet. You're putting him first and willing to do something that matters to him."

"You think so?" Kelsey asked. "I mean, I'm going to suck at it."

"How did he react?" Paige heard herself ask.

Kelsey looked over and shrugged. "He was thrilled, actually." She looked back at her sister. "But it's not something he can *keep*, like this."

"It will be a memory." Paige frowned. Why did she keep talking? But when they all looked at her, she tipped her head. "It will. You show up with all his favorite snacks and a *Warriors of Easton* sweatshirt and hat on to show him that you're really committed to doing it right and truly settle in for the whole weekend, no interruptions. He'll think that's super hot."

Then she winced. Oops, maybe she shouldn't tell teenagers how to be hot.

But Whitney, Josie, and Jane were nodding.

"It's true," Josie said. "Our parents were all about making the little things sweet and romantic." She shot Paige a smile. "Memories really matter. They *do* stay with you."

Oh crap, Paige thought as Josie looked at her with what could have easily been described as pride. She was right. And her sappy, romance-crazy parents had rubbed off on her after all.

Dammit.

"I need to go." She looked around. "Up front."

At least up front she wouldn't be opening her mouth in front of Josie and acting like she actually thought about romantic weekends and knew how to make things special and meaningful.

Paige took a deep breath and pushed through the swinging door to the front of the bakery. She immediately found Mitch in spite of the crowd of people.

I'd play stupid video games with him all weekend. For sure. Or go out on fishing boats on the swamp.

Dammit.

It seemed that he sensed her as well. He was sitting closest to the window at their table, not facing the kitchen door, but he looked over as soon as she stepped out. Their eyes met, and his mouth curled in a grin that sent heat skittering through her body. It was a knowing smile. A smile that said he knew her. Knew her body. Knew her thoughts. Knew that she would be here.

That idea made trepidation slip down her spine.

Turn around and go right back out of here. That was her first thought. Her first instinct.

But then he gave her a wink and leaned over, draping his arm across the back of the chair where Tori sat.

For some reason, that made Paige relax. So Josh and Tori were playing along? That was nice. And awkward. She felt bad. Her crazy family, and her own crazy commitment issues were causing Tori and Josh and Mitch to have to lie.

She sighed and made her way from behind the counter over to their table.

"Good morning."

"Paige!" Tori bounced up from her chair and hugged Paige. "Hi!"

Paige squeezed her back with a huge smile. Tori Kramer, soon-to-be-Landry, was impossible not to like. She was sweet and kind and genuine and slightly awkward in a very adorable I-just-want-to-take-care-of-her way.

Over Tori's shoulder, Paige noticed Josh watching them. He was smiling with an affectionate look that, if anyone had been looking, would have *clearly* said he was madly in love with Tori.

Paige let Tori go and grinned at her. "It's so good to see you. But I didn't know you were going to come over for the festival."

"Oh, it's the perfect reason to come see you," Tori said, taking her seat again. "When Mitch said that he was—"

"When he said how much he missed her but that he needed to stay to make sure all the electrical worked once things kicked off, Tori wanted to head right over," Josh interrupted, sitting forward.

Tori pressed her lips together and nodded, glancing at Mitch. "Right," she said. Then giggled. "I couldn't stay away from him another day though."

"Aw, love you, Tori," Mitch said. Then he pulled her in and kissed her.

It was just a quick peck on the lips, and his grin was full of mischief, but Josh's grin fell away and his body tensed.

Tori blushed.

Paige thought about knocking the rest of Mitch's coffee into his lap.

Ten

Of course, *all* of those reactions were what Mitch was going for.

"Dammit, Mitch," Josh muttered, too low for anyone else to hear.

But Mitch was focused on Paige. And she realized that he was trying to see how she'd react.

With jealousy. That's how she was reacting.

With stupid, makes-no-sense-because-she-knew-it-was-a-lie jealousy. Even more, she couldn't feel jealous over a guy that she didn't want anything long-term with. That was her call. That was her rule. That was her decision. She couldn't be jealous over other women or how he spent his time or if he didn't text or call her every day.

Even *more*, she *never* felt jealous. That was the truth. She had never met, dated, kissed, or even had a hookup with a guy she felt jealous about over anything.

She was going to have to get a handle on her emotions about *this* guy.

And it was definitely a red flag that her emotions were not handled even when she knew that he was just messing around.

Paige made herself sit back in her chair, cross her legs, and smile.

"Got to sell it," Mitch said to his cousin.

"I'm keepin' track," Josh told him. "I'm going to make you pay for *every* one of those."

"I'm so sorry," Paige said. She kept her voice low too. The bakery was busy and there was a lot of noise, but this was Appleby. It sometimes felt like the walls and trees even had ears. "He's helping me out and I realize it's ridiculous."

"It's fine," Tori said. "We've all got each other's backs. Mitch told us what was up before we even headed over here." She gave Josh a look. "You have nothing to worry about."

Josh nodded and gave her a wink. Then he leaned in and took Paige's hand in his on top of the table. "So, how are things at the yoga-cat café?"

Paige was surprised by the hand holding but she slid a glance at Mitch, knowing immediately what was going on. Mitch was looking at his cousin with his eyebrow arched.

Paige leaned in, closer to Josh too, feeling a touch of that same mischief that was in the air. "It's good. Very... relaxing."

Josh grinned and Paige completely understood what Tori saw in him. He was very good looking, but even more, he had a confident, laid-back charm about him that was definitely appealing.

"I mentioned she should look into otter yoga," Mitch said from across the table.

Josh's brows both arched. "You have otters?"

She laughed. "No."

"But *we* do," Mitch said.

Josh nodded. "Ah. Got it. Is that something you could do?" he asked Paige.

She shrugged. "I'd have to learn a lot about otters."

"Otters are not going to lie still and just stretch out like the cats," Tori said. "They're pretty active. If your yoga class is distracted by the otters, they won't be getting much meditation done."

Paige laughed. "Noted."

"Now, now," Mitch said. He moved his hand to rest it across Tori's shoulders rather than on the chair.

His big hand resting on the other woman made Paige's eyes narrow and she had to tell herself to relax.

"Let's not talk her out of things before we give it a fair try. I told her about the otter encounter and just said there wasn't a yoga studio in Autre. Let's not get excited about what *won't* work."

Josh looked interested in his cousin's interest in yoga. He slid his chair closer to Paige's.

Mitch's eyes followed the movement and he did the same, sliding closer to Tori.

Paige almost grinned. Tori laughed lightly.

"Well, how do you feel about alpacas?" she asked. "We're taking four back with us."

Paige did laugh then, sharing a look with Mitch. "Four?"

Tori grinned. "We went to talk to Drew. The one he thought I should take back with me is just a baby. An orphan. His mom died about a month ago. They've been bottle-feeding him but they don't really have the time to give him."

Drew and his brother Dallas were young bachelor farmers. They raised the alpacas for their wool. They weren't doing it because they wanted to spend all their time being fill-in moms, she was sure. They were nice guys but they had a huge farm to run, and whenever they had a runt kitten or found a stray, they called Paige rather than caring for it themselves.

"So, of course, they thought of you," Paige teased.

She and Tori had absolutely bonded over their love of animals, especially cats. Tori had told her that she'd been called Cinderella in elementary school after her classmates found out she'd had a pet racoon, rabbits, even mice. All animals liked her. And vice versa. When she'd lived in Iowa, she'd collected "special needs" animals, including a pig that was afraid of thunder, an English bulldog that had been born with a cleft palate and had needed to be fed by hand, and a mountain lion she'd saved after it had been shot as a cub, along with a few "regular" animals like goats and dogs and a whole bunch of cats. She'd even had an alpaca that loved it when she sang to him. Paige had no reason to believe that the sweet veterinarian was any different now just because she lived in Louisiana. And clearly Josh was very willing to indulge her.

"So what about the other three alpacas?" Paige asked.

"Well, I said…" Tori's cheeks got pink and she looked at Josh.

Paige looked at Josh too. The guy who was holding *her* hand. He was looking at Tori like he thought she was fucking adorable and hot as hell all at once.

"One of them came up and kissed her on the cheek," Josh said.

"Come on," Paige said with a laugh.

"Well, pretty much," Josh said. "Saw her across the pen and came straight over and put his mouth on her cheek. She, of course, was smitten. Then *his* girlfriend had to come. And their baby girl. Which, if things go well, will maybe be the other little llama's girlfriend someday, right?" he asked Tori.

Tori smiled at him like she thought *he* was adorable and hot as well.

Paige rolled her eyes. She hoped no one in the bakery was *really* paying attention because no way would they not realize these two wanted to tear each other's clothes off and sit on the porch in their rocking chairs at age ninety together.

Paige looked at Mitch. He was watching *her*. It made her feel warm and she smiled at him. Even though she knew that her smile didn't look casual to anyone looking on either. It was mostly tear-his-clothes-off. But there might have been a touch of rocking chair in there.

Dammit.

"Tell her about the whole plan," Mitch said to Tori. He picked up a strand of her hair and twirled it around his finger.

Josh shifted to put his arm around Paige.

"Well," Tori said, her eyes on Josh's arm. "We're starting a whole petting zoo and animal encounter as an offshoot of Boys of the Bayou."

"We're calling it Boys of the Bayou Gone Wild," Josh said. He grinned. "Totally tongue-in-cheek since otters and alpacas aren't very wild."

Paige laughed. "I love it." She looked at Tori. "That sounds like your kind of thing, for sure."

"Yeah, otters and alpacas and goats and my pot-bellied pig and who knows what else." Tori said with a smile. "But I'm not doing it. I mean, most of the petting zoo animals are mine and I'll help out, but a friend of mine from vet school has joined me in my practice and Gone Wild will be his thing. And we still need someone to run that part of the business. Josh and Owen and Sawyer don't have time. That's where Mitch comes in."

Paige looked at Mitch. He shook his head.

"I'm just building pens and things."

"No you're not. You're going to be great managing it," Tori said, pivoting on her chair to look at him more fully. "You're going to do what Josh and Owen do on the boats."

Mitch grinned and looked at his cousin. "I don't know what you're talkin' about."

Tori rolled her eyes. "Uh-huh." She looked at Paige. "The Boys of the Bayou is a fantastic tour of the bayou with a lot of information and great experiences built in. They talk about the plants and animals of the bayou as well as the history and legends of the area. They make sure the tourists see alligators and other animals in the wild, and they take them to see some of the old cabins and talk about the people who settled the area. It's a great tour. But..." She cast another affectionate glance at her fiancé.

"But?" Paige asked, looking from Josh to Tori.

"But the *boys* of the bayou are a huge draw. Josh and Owen and even Sawyer are a part of the fabulous reviews. They flirt. They talk hunting and fishing. They turn on the Southern charm and those drawls."

Paige nodded, but she was looking at Mitch now. "I know exactly what you're talking about."

Tori laughed. "Yep. The women think they're hot and charming when they're teasing and flirting, and it's really weird how often the guys end up shirtless and wet."

"Hmm, that is really *weird*," Paige said sarcastically to Josh.

He just grinned.

"And the men think they're cool. They drive airboats and hunt alligators and all kinds of manly man stuff." Tori rolled her eyes again, but she was still smiling.

Paige shook her head, fighting her own smile. "That does sound pretty cool."

Josh nodded. "And then there's how great we are with kids." He looked at his fiancé. "Admit it. That makes your panties melt, Iowa."

Tori didn't answer right away, but she didn't deny it either.

Paige knew that guys interacting well with children were a lust button for a lot of women. A lot of her friends, for that matter.

"So you're going to manage the petting zoo and otter encounter?" she asked Mitch. She wasn't going to think about him with kids. That didn't work with her. She had nieces and nephews. She liked kids fine, but she wasn't ga-ga over babies or little kids, and her biological clock wasn't even wound up not to mention ticking.

"No. I'm building the pens and enclosures," he said again. He gave Tori a look.

She sighed. "You'd be so good."

"You want me puttin' up fences with my shirt off?" he asked, giving her a small smile. "I can do that."

He should *absolutely* do that. And charge admission, for sure, Paige thought.

But she noted his smile seemed forced.

Interesting. He didn't want to be more involved with the animal portion of the business? Why not?

"Well, *at least* that," Tori teased. "You'd just be so good talking about the animals. You love them. And you're as charming and sweet and funny as Josh and Owen."

"Hey, now," Josh said. But his tone was light.

Tori shot him a smile. "You know what I mean. All the charm you turn on for the tourists. Mitch can do that. I'm not talking about the you-and-me charm."

The way she said *charm* made Paige's eyes widen. It looked like the sweet, small-town farmgirl had been a little corrupted by the Louisiana boy who was now giving her hot looks over sweet, small-town muffins and coffee.

Paige glanced at Mitch. She understood that. She really did. She wanted to be a little corrupted herself.

"There's no other charm like that, babe," Josh said, his voice dropping low.

"Okay," Paige said, squeezing Josh's hand to remind him not to eye-fuck Tori across the table in the bakery.

Tori fanned her face and gave Josh a wink, but she said to Mitch, "And you love the otters. Admit it."

"Otters are cute." Mitch shrugged. "Everyone likes otters."

Tori blew out a breath.

"I've got Fletcher and Zeke helping me," Mitch said. "They can take care of the tourists."

"His mom specifically told me we're supposed to call him Ezekiel," Tori said with a grin.

Mitch and Josh both laughed. Mitch looked at Paige. "Zeke's one of my cousins. Fletcher too. But Zeke and Zander are twins. Their mom hates that we shorten Ezekiel and Alexander."

"But the family's been doing it all their lives and they're twenty-six," Josh said. "You'd think she'd be used to it by now."

Tori shook her head. "I think she was hoping that since I'm kind of new, she could at least get me to do it right." She looked at Paige. "In the Landry family, the *more* something bugs you, the more likely it's going to continue. You have to learn to roll with things on the bayou."

Paige couldn't deny she was fascinated.

The conversation about Mitch's role with the tourists had gotten sidetracked. She was pretty sure he'd intended that, but the whole topic seemed to be an ongoing discussion. Paige wanted to ask him more about it later. Then realized that it was none of her business what Mitch did with his job and his family's business. If he didn't want to do more, that was his choice. She didn't know what that was about and it didn't matter.

Paige opened her mouth to ask a question when suddenly there was a murmuring in the crowd and the sound of chairs scraping and people started to pivot in the same direction.

Paige frowned and looked as well.

"I know we haven't known each other very long, but I'm absolutely crazy about you."

Elliot, one of the programmers who worked for Aiden, Grant, Cam, and Oliver, the guys who had bought the Hot Cakes factory, was standing in front of the bakery case. He was facing his boyfriend, Max, one of the factory workers, who everyone in town adored.

Max's eyes were wide and his mouth was hanging open.

"When I bid on you at the bachelor auction, I knew we were going to have fun," Elliot said. "But I had no idea what I was *actually* winning." He dropped to one knee in front of Max. "A chance at everything I've always wanted." He was holding a red velvet cupcake in one hand and a gold band in the other. "Max, will you marry me?"

The entire bakery sucked in a breath all at once and not a single person moved.

Including Max.

He just stood staring down at his boyfriend.

Paige felt herself leaning forward. Holy shit, was Max going to turn him down in front of everyone?

But Elliot didn't look nervous. He just waited.

Finally Jane coughed from behind the counter. Her cough sounded like, "*Max.*"

Max shook his head. "Elliot."

Elliot just kept the ring extended.

"Fuck, yes," Max said, shaking his head slowly. "Damn."

Elliot gave him a huge smile and got to his feet.

The big, burly man grabbed Elliot and pulled him into his arms, hugging him tightly.

The whole bakery cheered, and Jane came rushing around the bakery case to throw her arms around both men.

Paige tried to swallow and found that her throat was tight. She blinked fast. What the hell? Were her eyes a little watery?

She sat back in her chair and glanced over at Mitch. He was watching her with a smile. She rolled her eyes at him. He laughed.

"Oh my gosh!" Tori said, then gave a happy sigh. "That was amazing. Do you know them?" she asked Paige.

"I know Max," Paige said. "Elliot is from Chicago. They just met this past summer."

"When you know, you know," Mitch said simply.

She frowned at him. "Watch yourself, Bayou."

Josh laughed at that. "He can't help it. He's a Landry."

"What's that mean?" Paige asked, not sure she really wanted to know.

"The Landrys have a long, proud history of big romance," Josh said, almost smugly.

Paige groaned.

Josh chuckled. "That's a bad thing?

"Don't scare her off before I get her down there and can seduce her with beignets," Mitch said.

"Romance scares you off?" Tori asked.

Paige glanced over to where Max and Elliot were accepting congratulations and she couldn't help but smile.

"I'm not sure scared is the right word," she admitted.

"That's my girl," Mitch said gruffly from across the table.

"Maybe you just haven't—" Tori started but she gave a little, "*Eek*," and then pressed her lips together.

Paige assumed Mitch had pinched her or something.

Well, good. At least he was getting the message not to *talk about it* all the damned time, no matter how he felt.

"Paige is gonna be my 'plus one' at your wedding," Mitch told Tori, his eyes on Paige.

She should say no.

If she went to Louisiana she might not make it to Colorado.

"Oh *yes*," Tori exclaimed, her eyes bright. "I was going to invite you anyway. Please come. Mitch will make sure you have fun." Then she giggled. "I didn't mean it like that but..."

"Okay, Tor," Mitch said with a grin. "Paige knows what you meant."

Paige didn't care what Tori meant. She was concerned about what *Mitch* meant.

"It will be a ton of fun. You'll love Autre and everyone," Josh said. "Please come."

Everyone. She was going to meet everyone.

The big, romantic everyone.

Ugh.

Paige looked back and forth between Tori and Josh. They were such nice people. Then she looked at Mitch. Then over at Max and Elliot and then at Kelsey who was standing with Josie and Grant and Zoe and Aiden wearing her new heart necklace.

Everyone was freaking in love.

There was romance and wedding stuff everywhere she looked.

She blew out a breath. Escaping sounded great, but escaping by going to a *wedding* in another little town with a whole bunch of people who loved love seemed like kind of the opposite thing she should do.

But then she looked at Mitch.

She wasn't ready to say goodbye to him yet.

Crap.

She felt herself nodding. "Yeah, okay, I'll come to the wedding."

Mitch's smile was definitely pleased. But also a little knowing.

She was going to have to limit the texting and calls between now and the wedding. She didn't want him to get the idea that they were *dating* or had a serious relationship going into that romantic weekend.

And she was only staying for a couple of days. Tops.

Twenty minutes later, they were wandering through the town square, stopping at every single booth.

They sampled hot cider—that was very hot thanks to the electricity flowing into the booth—and caramel apples and mini apple pies from Buttered Up and apple cookies and applesauce and even apple wine. It was all homemade and, frankly, delicious.

Most people claimed they wouldn't touch another apple recipe for weeks after leaving the square but that never ended up being true.

They also checked out the craft stations where you could paint with apple cores and get a temporary apple tattoo along with the booths where people were selling everything from wooden apples to ceramic apples to towels embroidered with apples.

"Wow," Mitch said when they were through the square and on their way to the yoga studio so Tori could take a look at the cats. "I mean, when you people adopt a theme, you go all in."

Paige laughed. "For sure."

"Oh, you bayou boys can't talk," Tori said. "There are alligators on everything in Autre."

"The bayou is a way of life," Josh told her. "We have to celebrate it."

Mitch nodded his agreement.

After Tori checked over all the cats, which took a while considering all the ooh-ing and ahh-ing and cuddling that went on while she examined them, Mitch finally got to his feet.

"Guess we're heading out," he said.

Paige looked up, then scrambled to her feet. "Oh. Really? Today?"

Today was the day they were supposed to *arrive*.

But it was fine they were leaving. This was the amount of time she'd expected to spend with Mitch. Short and sweet. No big deal.

So why did it feel like so much had happened and that his visit had been a very big deal?

"Yeah, we need to get back," he said, shooting a glance at Tori.

"I'm sorry," Tori said. "It's my fault."

"It's *my* fault," Josh said. "I should have known taking her over to the Ryan farm was the wrong move."

"But I wanted to meet everybody," Tori said.

"Everybody being the alpaca—the *one* alpaca—that she was supposed to be taking back to Louisiana," Mitch added.

"And now it's four alpacas," Paige said with a smile.

Tori nodded.

"And…" Mitch said.

Paige looked at her with wide eyes. "There's more?"

"There was a donkey," Tori said, lifting her shoulder.

"Who now belongs to us too," Josh said.

Paige shook her head. "Wow."

Tori said, lifting a shoulder. "Drew asked if I wanted him."

Mitch laughed. "And Tori's never met an animal she *doesn't* want."

"Anyway," Josh said, "now that she's met her new babies, she wants to get them home and settled."

Paige wondered if Josh *ever* said no to Tori. But she couldn't help smiling. Clearly they were both incredibly happy.

She looked up at Mitch. And now she was going to get rid of him sooner. Before she started liking him any more than she already did.

"I am sorry to be taking Mitch back to Louisiana so soon though," Tori said, truly looking regretful. "But we do need his help with the trailers and driving that far straight through and everything."

"It's fine," Paige assured her.

Mitch lifted a brow as if to ask *it is, huh?*

Well, it *should* be. He was just some guy she'd met and had some sexy fun with. Hell, he already knew more about her life than the last three guys she'd "dated". It was time for him to go.

But she was going to miss him.

She wasn't able to quite avoid that thought entirely.

"I need to grab my stuff from upstairs," he said to her. "Come with me."

There was not a question mark at the end of that sentence. Still, she nodded.

"I didn't realize you'd left your stuff up there," she said as she led him up the stairs.

"You thought I took it all to the bakery with me?" he asked.

"I didn't know you went to the bakery."

"Where did you think I went?"

"Louisiana."

She pushed the door open and stepped inside.

He grabbed her wrist and swung her around. He wrapped an arm around her waist and brought her in for a deep kiss.

Her hands slid into his hair, and she went up on tiptoe to get closer.

This is what I'm going to miss she told herself. *All I'm going to miss.*

You're a freaking liar herself said right back.

When he let her go she was breathing hard.

"I've been dying to do that all morning," he said.

She nodded. Hanging out at the bakery and watching him pretend to be with Tori—and being stupidly jealous of it—had been bad enough, but walking through the square and watching him hold Tori's hand and feed her bites of cookie and brush glitter out of her hair had been irritating. Even though it was all fake. And she didn't want any of that herself.

It was definitely good he was leaving.

He was cupping her cheek and watching her. "I'll see you in thirty-eight days," he said.

Her eyes widened. "Thirty-eight days? That's not even two months."

He grinned. "Exactly."

"Are you coming back here for some reason?" Her heart thumped. She tried to tell herself it was because that idea made her nervous. But she was starting to think that she was not only a liar, but a pretty bad one.

"Do you want me to come back before then? I'll be here. Just say the word," he told her gruffly.

She wanted to say that word. Kind of. More than she did with anyone else anyway.

"Though you'll have to somehow explain that to your mom."

That would be interesting.

"I just... I mean..."

He finally chuckled. "Relax. I'm just giving you shit, you gorgeous commitment-phobe. The wedding is in thirty-eight days."

She pulled back. "What? That means they're getting married in February."

She'd assumed the wedding would be in the spring. Or June. Like a normal wedding time. Several months in the future.

Why was nothing with this guy going according to plan?

"They're getting married on Mardi Gras," he said. "That's when they met and when they got back together. So they almost have to." He shrugged.

"Mardi Gras is in *February*?"

Why didn't she know that? Why did Mardi Gras seem like a warm-weather event? Probably all the naked boobs associated with the holiday. Then again, it *was* a warm-weather event since it was mostly celebrated in the South. February in Louisiana was definitely warmer than February in Iowa.

Which was a major draw to this wedding for this Iowa girl.

As if the big guy who was dragging his hand down the side of her body and settling it on her hip wasn't enough.

He is. He so is. And don't even try to lie about it.

Yeah, yeah.

"Well, I guess I'll see you soon, then," she said.

He laughed and leaned in and kissed her before letting her go. "You need to work on acting enthusiastic about that before you get there, okay? My ego can only take so much."

She grinned a genuine grin. "I'm not worried about your ego."

It was probably a good thing he was sure of himself and cocky. He could handle her less-than-enthusiastic quirks about intimacy and commitment better than most men. The guys around here got their feelings hurt pretty easily. It was another reason she rarely said yes to dates with guys from Appleby. She mostly dated guys from other towns... the bigger and farther away, the better.

Mitch would be the farthest away of any guy she'd dated though—if that's what they were going to call it—and that didn't feel like a perk, exactly.

He pulled her in close again and put his mouth against her ear. "I can't wait to see you and have you for six months straight."

She felt tingles racing through her body and she had to focus on what he'd said. "You said six *days* last night," she reminded him. And she hadn't agreed to that. Yet.

"Okay, fine, we'll compromise at six weeks."

"I can't." Well, she *shouldn't*. She *could*. Technically, she supposed.

He kissed her, then lifted his head. "We'll see."

"That should sound creepy. Like you're going to lock me up or something."

He didn't grin. He cupped her face again. "*Does* it sound creepy?"

She wet her lips and then said honestly, "No."

"We'll take it... six days at a time," he said.

She smiled. "You don't take no for an answer very easily."

"Actually, I'm pretty easy going about most things. Usually. But I've never wanted something this much." His gaze was still serious and she felt her stomach flip. He dragged his thumb over her bottom lip. "But I won't push you."

"You'll just *tempt* me?" she asked.

"Oh yes. That. For sure." Now the slow, sexy smile curled his mouth.

"Thanks for the warning."

He stepped back after another long look. Then he grabbed his bag from beside the door.

How had she not noticed that before? Well, she'd been on the phone with her sister, panicking about Tori and Josh and Mitch being at Buttered Up.

Mitch pulled the door open and looked back. "See ya soon."

She nodded. "Yeah."

He smiled and then left.

As the door shut behind him, only one thought went through her head.

I already miss him.

Well, fu... fudge.

Eleven

One week later...

Josie and Grant's wedding was easily the most romantic thing Paige had ever witnessed.

Of course it was. It was Josie. The most in-love-with-love person Paige had ever met. And that included their own parents and grandparents.

Josie looked gorgeous, even with tears—happy tears, of course—streaming down her face. Grant had even choked up during his vows.

The flowers were gorgeous. The music was gorgeous. Josie's dress was gorgeous. Hell, even the bridesmaids' dresses—Paige, Zoe, Jane, and Amanda wore—were gorgeous. And when did that ever happen?

The cake was, of course, *gorgeous*. Zoe and Josie had made it themselves, and Paige had to admit, it was a work of art.

Paige tipped back her glass of champagne. Her first, but she intended to keep the free booze flowing. They were at the reception now, and she didn't have to make a speech—that was Zoe's job as maid of honor—so Paige could definitely get drunk.

She really wanted to get drunk.

She was surrounded by in-love people. Her sister and Grant. Zoe and Aiden. Jane and Dax. Whitney and Cam. Max and Elliot. Even Kelsey was here with Matt, freaking *glowing* as they danced.

The worst part though, was that her and Josie's parents and grandparents and aunts and uncles and, well, *everyone*, were so, so happy. No, it wasn't bad that they were happy. She didn't begrudge them that. But it did remind her that they were still sad about the Wedding Reception That Never Was.

Aka, Paige's fuckup.

They were learning though, because only two people—and neither relatives of hers—had commented that it was her turn next. So she only needed to add two cats to her collection.

Of course, part of being around her extended family at a *wedding,* of all things, was she knew they were all whispering to one another about how "too bad" it was that the handsome, charming man she'd been holding hands with in the bakery last week lived so far away. What they really meant was that it was typical that Paige would finally show some interest in someone and he'd be out of reach. But Josie telling them all that Josh was from Louisiana and he owned his own business there, and, no, there was no way he could move to Iowa, did keep them from bugging Paige about holding his hand in public.

Paige set the champagne glass down and sighed.

And admitted the *actual* worst part.

She wished that Mitch were here.

And not just because then her Aunt Vivian would stop giving her pitying looks as she sat at the head table alone, the only single bridesmaid. She and Oliver, one of Grant's best friends, were the only two single members of the bridal party, period, and everyone knew Ollie was in love with Piper.

Well, everyone except Ollie himself.

Ollie and Piper were dancing now too.

Paige wished Mitch were here because she'd love to dance with him. And drink champagne. And flirt and laugh and tease and just have fun.

Mitch would be fun to be with.

At the dance. At the *wedding dance.*

She wouldn't even mind that her mother would be pleased and hopeful watching her and Mitch together. She might even smile and say, "We'll see" when her mother asked if he could be The One. Instead of her usual, "You just added another year of spinsterhood to my calendar. At this rate, I won't be married until I'm fifty."

Her mother would always roll her eyes and mutter something under her breath, and Paige couldn't quite hear but assumed was along the lines of "Where did I go wrong?" or "I need to stop for wine on the way home."

"Hi, Paige."

She looked up and blinked, pulling her attention away from her thoughts. "Oh, hi, Carter."

"Would you like to dance?"

She looked from Carter Rogers to the dance floor then back.

No, not really. Not unless Mitch was here.

But Mitch wasn't here, and it was her sister's wedding dance, and, as much as she hated to do it, it would make her mom happy.

She sighed. She didn't hate making her mom happy. She loved her mom. She just wished that making her happy didn't involve her getting hitched. She'd given her mother *plenty* of grandkids to spoil. They had fur and couldn't talk, but they also potty trained *really* easily and could be left alone when she went out, like to a wedding, without her having to pay a sitter.

"Paige?"

"Oh right." She smiled at Carter. Carter had been a classmate of hers and she'd always liked him. He was one of the smartest guys in their class and he'd gone off to college on a full scholarship. He'd just moved back and started his business. Something about bringing up-and-coming tech to rural areas of the Midwest.

She was sure he was going to be successful. And in Appleby for the rest of his life.

"Sure," she finally said. They could *dance* though.

He led her to the dance floor and she let him pull her close. It wasn't her fault that she instantly began comparing being against him to being against Mitch.

But as they danced she relaxed.

They talked and laughed. She'd forgotten Carter was funny. She hadn't forgotten that he was cute and they got along well though. She was glad he'd asked her to dance.

She participated in the bouquet toss—dodging the stupid thing when her sister practically threw it right to her. Carter took part in the garter toss. They did the "Hokey Pokey" and line danced to "Achy Breaky Heart".

And when the dance was over, she let him walk her out to her car. She would have walked all the way home if it weren't for her heels and fancy dress and the sixteen-degree wind chill. Why her sister had wanted to get married in January was beyond her.

"This was fun," Carter said, pulling her door open.

"It was," Paige agreed. See? Why couldn't people just hang out and have fun without it meaning more?

"I've been thinking about you since I moved back," Carter said.

Paige froze. *No.* No, no, no.

"What do you mean?"

He smiled. And it did *nothing* to her stomach.

"I was really glad you were still single when I got back," he said.

Paige tossed her purse onto the passenger seat with a sigh. Well, dammit.

"I'm not looking for a boyfriend, Carter," she said.

He moved in closer. "Well, good. Because I don't want to be your boyfriend."

Paige narrowed her eyes. Was he thinking about a fling? She

might have considered that, but... Mitch had happened. And now she wasn't attracted to Carter at all.

"Then what do you want?" she asked, not wanting to assume anything here.

"We're both living and working here, settling down," Carter said. "We're at the same place in our lives. I think we should get married."

Paige wondered for a moment if she'd had more champagne than she'd thought. But no. This was happening.

"You're not even going to take me out to dinner?" she asked with an eye roll. "Pretend to work up to this?"

In one way, in the back part of her brain, she kind of appreciated the no-nonsense, skip the romantic bullshit approach.

That didn't, however, make her appreciate that she was being *proposed to. Again.* For fuck's sake.

Did she have a sign on her forehead? Had her mother signed her up on an online dating site with a description that read "Ready to marry immediately. Serious offers only"?

Actually, that last one made a little sense, and Paige made a mental note to check those sites tomorrow.

"Of course I'll take you to dinner," Carter said. "Anything you want. But I just don't think we should beat around the bush. I want you to know that I'm serious about this. I'm ready to make a commitment."

Otter yoga.

Those were the two words that went through her head.

She had to get out of here.

And there was really only one place she could even consider going.

"Well, that's not really going to work for me," she said, pushing Carter back and getting into the car.

"What? Why not? I've asked around. You've dated pretty much everyone here. If something was going to happen with someone here, it would have, don't you think?"

She nodded. "Absolutely."

"So what's the problem?"

"Well, gosh, for one... I don't want to marry you." She reached for the door and pulled it partially shut. Then she added. "For another, I'm leaving in the morning." Sure, it was a month early, but the idea of showing up in Autre, Louisiana and surprising Mitch made her heart pound.

"Leaving?" Carter asked, clearly confused.

"Yeah. I'm moving." She sounded completely confident. And happy. And she maybe *felt* both of those things too. "Away from Appleby."

"Where are you going? My grandma didn't say anything about that," Carter said with a frown.

It was actually fair, sadly, for Carter to assume his grandmother would know all about any plans like that.

Paige smiled at her fifth proposal and said with relief and a sense of anticipation that she hadn't felt in... ever, "South. I need a break and a little... heat."

"Just south? That's all you know?"

"That's all *you* need to know."

"Is it a guy?" he asked with a frown.

She didn't answer right away. That would definitely get back to his grandmother, then to her grandmother, then to her mother...

But would that be so bad? She'd be out of state, away from here, away from the drop-ins to try to get information.

"Yeah, it is," she finally said.

"Wow," Carter said. "You must be in love."

"No," she said quickly. "It's not that."

"Paige," Carter said. "You've never so much as changed your pizza order for a guy. But now you're *moving* for one? If it's not love, what is it?"

Well, she... couldn't say for sure. But it *wasn't* love.

Was it?

Was this what falling in love felt like?

Oh... fu... *fuck*.

~

Want to know what happens once Paige gets to Louisiana? Yes, there's more of their story!

You can see it *all* in Mitch and Paige's book, the full-length novel in the Boys of the Bayou series, **Four Weddings and a Swamp Boat Tour**

Charming, sexy bayou boy Mitch Landry gets stuff done. Whatever anyone needs. From alligator-sitting to getting a buddy drunk to showing a woman a good time to fixing a swamp boat, he's the man. No problem. No drama.

But he wants a hell of a lot more from Paige than a temporary friends-with-benefits arrangement. He wants to take care of her. And her five cats. He also really wants other men to stop asking her to marry them.

But if a roommate and a few orgasms are all she wants, that's what he'll deliver.

He can just be her friend and not commit the greatest sin of all... asking her for forever.

Probably.

~

Next up in the Hot Cakes series is Ollie and Piper in the funny, sexy, friends-to-lover, boss-assistant romance, *Gimme S'more!*

~

<u>The Hot Cakes Series</u>
Sugarcoated (Aiden and Zoe)
Forking Around (Dax and Jane)
Making Whoopie (Grant and Josie)
Semi-Sweet On You (Cam and Whitney)
Oh, Fudge (Paige and Mitch)
Gimme S'more (Ollie and Piper)

Find all my books, including a printable book list, at
www.ErinNicholas.com

~

And join in on all the FAN FUN!

The best place to find out all the news is right here:
bit.ly/Keep-In-Touch-Erin
(be sure you get those capital letters and dashes in there!)

And this is your personal invitation to my Facebook group, Erin Nicholas's Super Fans where you can get first looks, behind the scenes peeks, and daily fun with fellow romance lovers (including me!)!